MW01113322

A Novel

Theodore James Putala

For my mother,

Claire White Putala,

and my father,

Eugene C. Putala,

With deepest gratitude.

Nothing is by coincidence.

CHAPTER ONE

It was already two minutes after ten. I'd stayed up reading a story, started thinking about girls and fallen asleep.

I splashed some water on my face, brushed my teeth, threw a shirt on and jogged up the grassy hill below the art museum. I was about the only one out for a walk. There was a guy turning his mower over the grass up on the quad.

The classroom was in a two-story building of mortared granite block, square with the lines of a barn. I pulled the outer door open, the opening lecture muffled at the end of the hardwood hallway.

"Certain people have the ability to see ghosts," Duchamp was saying just as I bumbled in.

The door creaked behind me as I closed it. Daylight came in through the windows, everyone quiet. I slid over to my chair in the back.

"Mr. Tarnowski knows how to make an entrance," Duchamp said from the desk at the front of the classroom. He had been my advisor freshman year, picking me out of the entering class, for something I'd writtten. "I worry about you sometimes, Mr. T.," he said as I got settled. He'd just come back after a yearlong sabbatical.

The Princess sat two rows ahead of me on my left by the middle window. A pencil rolled off her notebook onto the floor and she reached down to pick it up. She placed the pencil back on her desk and then her pen rolled off. I'd seen her the first time at a party that fall dancing with a friend of mine. She saw me looking around on the carpet for the key she'd lost. I saw her sitting there the first day of class back in January and again it was that awkward beautiful thing at first sight.

"Act One, Scene One," Duchamp called out, looking down into his book. "We have Horatio here, like our model Amherst student: skeptical, reasonable, and charming, let's not forget."

I jotted a note in the margin of the page.

"*Th' extravagant and erring spirit hies / To his confine…*" He turned to the Princess. "Miss Dorfmann, what sort of verbal behavior is this here?"

Sitting up straight, she spoke in a clear high voice like a sound coming to you at dusk. "By explaining the ghost, Horatio's taking the shock out of seeing it, so that it doesn't take on its own meaning."

"Very good."

"You wouldn't want the ghost stealing the scene, would you, if you were Horatio," she added.

"Horatio's reference point—as Miss Dorfmann has given us--is that all experience is legible. There are no mysteries. Everything under the sun has a perfectly reasonable explanation." Duchamp looked around, peering out from his brow as he leaned forward, his ears prominent, pointed almost beneath youthful wisps of hair, his hands crossed, fingers intertwined. "Act One, Scene Two. King Claudius addresses the court. Miss Horner, read for us the King here, from *take thy fair hour…*"

"*And thy best graces spend it as thy will. But now, my cousin Hamlet and my son,*" Eva Horner said, reading slowly, in a voice I found just slightly too high.

"Well done," Duchamp said. "The King is moving how?"

"Turning to face Hamlet."

"Oh, Lord. He's biting the bullet here. And then we get Hamlet in this next speech. His mother tries to coax him out of his mood... *Seems, madam?* Mr. Tarnowski, give us this speech."

I cleared my throat and read Hamlet's speech carefully, in a low voice. I needed a drink of water. "*Seems, madam? Nay, it is. I know not 'seems.' / 'Tis not alone my inky cloak, good mother, / Nor customary suits of solemn black, / Nor windy suspiration of forced breath, / No, nor the fruitful river in the eye, / Nor the dejected havior of the visage, / Together with all forms, moods, shapes of grief, / That can denote me truly. These indeed seem, / For they are actions that a man might play, / But I have that within,*" I paused, my voice thickening, wondering if I'd read too much, "*which passeth show-- / These are but the trappings and suits of woe.*"

"Almost a technical knock-out. Thank you, Mr. Tarnowski. Describe for us this as a response to the King."

"Well, for Hamlet there's not this distance. It's like he's saying he doesn't have the leisure to be so cunning."

Duchamp looked out over our heads, just like the pose in the dust jacket photo of him in an old book my mother found for me, a novel he had written. A handsome man with big features and a rugged frame, he looked like someone who'd have fought in the Revolutionary War alongside General

Washington. A few weeks before he'd been telling us about burying the loyal old family dog with his father when suddenly he let out a loud animal sob, a single moan, in the middle of class. No one said anything about it later, as if they didn't care to notice. But the girl, she looked down gently after, filing it away somewhere in a world which was a surprise.

The clock on the wall above the door ticked, the second hand sweeping past twelve. A cloud passed and the light outside came bright across the pines again. Duchamp turned a few pages in silence.

"Now, Act Four, Scene Five. *Enter Ophelia (distracted).* Line 41. *How do you, pretty lady?* Fatherly, human, a touch of shame and sorrow. *Conceit upon her father.* Meditative."

I was reading along, looking over Ophelia's song about Saint Valentine's Day, not exactly paying perfect attention.

"Mr. Tarnowski, give us the King here. Line 56, *Pretty Ophelia!*"

"Pity," I said quietly. "He has some sympathy now."

"Yes," the man said evenly. "Give us more."

"The King is getting back in touch with his emotions."

"Yes. The King is moving from his life as an institution to his life as an individual, back to personal terms and the necessity for self-awareness. There is a spirit of tenderness here as the King looks at Ophelia."

The hour passed, the sun no longer in the windows. I closed my little book and watched Duchamp up at the front, towering with his broad chest over Miss Portnoy and her frizzy hair, leaving with her through the first door of the classroom. The Princess gathered her things into a woven straw shoulder bag. I stepped out the rear door of the room to the hallway. I hadn't taken a shower that morning.

I walked along a hedge, back in the air.

He'd written that nice poem to her. *Doubt thou the stars are fire, doubt truth to be a liar, but never doubt I love.* But that hadn't been enough.

I went back to my dorm room after a sandwich, a couple glasses of soda to quench my thirst and the usual dining hall banter. Sitting on the bed I took a moment to look up at the map of the Caribbean above the standard issue veneered desk by the one window, the seas an appropriate blue.

I took my baseball glove and the lacrosse ball down from the standing dresser. The leather baseball spikes I'd found in a vintage clothing store pinched my toes, but I liked them, the shiny black. I put my paint-spattered cap on and walked back through the bathroom, out the door and down the steps. I jogged out across the lawn in the direction of the athletic fields. Thin gray clouds were sweeping in quickly over the valley.

The Science Center rose before me, a dusty-pink brick bunker. On the downhill side facing the Social Dorms there was a slope with a half-dozen bare Norway Maples spaced evenly in the shade. I liked throwing the ball against the wall, grabbing it as it came back through the trees. I was good at it. The dense rubber of the lacrosse ball was heavy enough to give my throwing arm a workout.

I came up to the building, lobbing the ball against the wall. I took out the pouch of chewing tobacco. I warmed up steadily, stopping now and then to spit out the tobacco juice, all part of the necessary rhythm. The ball hit the wall, bouncing back over the grass. I chased it down as it came past me on the backhand side, turning to fire it back in time.

Jenny Havermeyer, captain of the tennis team, came strolling up the path from the courts. She had lived above my room group the year before.

I lofted the ball again, caught a back-hander. I had to pivot all the way around to throw it against the wall for the next bounce. I turned to look up at her face. She looked wonderful in her tennis wear, with the short skirt that showed off her long firm legs, her covered tennis racket resting playfully over her shoulder. The ball got away from me on a weird bounce, and I loped down the hill toward the walk to retrieve it, catching my breath.

"I'll never make the majors playing like that," I said, looking down, biting my lip as I scooped the ball up.

She laughed her sunny easy laugh, smiling as she walked on, her chin up, her feet so perfectly underneath her, the world seeming to wag pleasantly behind her as she walked away along the path. Maybe being from Chicago, a Hemingway Summer Person had something to do with it.

I turned and threw the ball low at the wall. It thumped against the brick and dribbled back to me, rolling along the grassy dirt. I stepped back to the mound to do some pitching, checking a runner at first.

Then the air changed and a light rain began to fall, carrying a hint of warmer weather, and I walked through it back to the dorm. Hume came jogging along, dressed for baseball practice. "You look just like *The Natural*, Jamie," he called out.

"Yeah, I could never hit though," I called after him, smiling. He'd already gone a ways.

I would go outside and throw a tennis ball in the driveway against the house. Ground balls, sometimes fly balls when I tossed the ball up high and it came back. When I threw it too close to where the kitchen was Mom would yell out for me to stop it, she couldn't take it anymore.

I could hit the ball pretty good in practice. I hit the ball beautifully a couple of times in bush league practice. Shannon's brother tossed me one and I took a swing and it went off straight over his head and deep. Shannon himself called out and I stopped on second base. "Damn," Shannon said. And I smiled and touched the bill of my cap. I'd hit a triple at least the week before but didn't run it because it was late. Shannon hadn't seen that. That had been the best, the longest I'd ever hit it. Maybe it was even a homer really, if a ballpark fence had been there on the school playground.

I'd done the same thing in Mr. Burlington's gym class back in sixth grade. He threw the ball in and I got the whole swing into it and drove it clean and clear straight toward left center. It surprised the hell out of Mr. Burlington. I was still swinging when it flew over his head. "Jesus," he said, turning quickly around, and he never said anything like that. I was surprised too. It was a shot. I just looked at it. It felt pretty good, getting hold of it like that, and it turned out after all to be surprisingly easy. I didn't have time to run really. I don't think I even dropped the bat. I just watched the ball sail away over everyone's head. Tim Bailey was playing way out deep in right center, like he didn't even want to be part of the game, wearing my glove even, and he caught it. He didn't even have to move, standing way out there by himself. He just lifted my old glove that my brother and I shared up and the ball went right in it. He just stood there. The ball in my glove, and there was almost this groan, passing across the field. It wasn't fair, the one big hit, a beauty. No one even said anything afterward.

I could never hit it in a real game. I tried. I kept my eye on the ball. I swung. I might have it hit foul once. I struck out and then I had to go back to whatever there was for a dugout, silence along the bench, the coach not even looking at me. Not in the park off of Utica Street, not in Clarks Mills. Shannon's brother suggested I try to bunt. He tried to tell me how to do it, but I guess I was half-hearted about it and it was just as hard anyway with everyone looking at you.

Once, I was playing third and caught a hot line drive. My mother was in the stands behind me, and I heard her, 'he caught it, he caught it.' Laughing almost. I never had any problem making a good catch or throwing even. In gym class there was a fly ball right toward Toby Peeps, who couldn't do anything, and I came running from center just as it came off the bat and I ran and I reached and got it just at the right moment. Nothing against Toby Peeps, just that everyone knew he couldn't and just stood there. "Hooray," they all went, even Hutch the gym coach.

But I could never hit in a real game, I don't know why. Maybe they threw me meatballs in gym class and baseball practice, figuring I was a wimp too and couldn't swing a bat. Those few magic hits though, they were big one. I had a good swing. I hit that ball.

I went out for a walk down in the woods after I did my reading. I liked walking at night, being outside. It did me good.

The forest was young, the trees straight and tall. I could see my breath in the moonlight. I came upon the clearing for the railroad bed. Standing on the gravel between the ties, I followed the empty tracks curving along a long bend until they disappeared. I stood for a moment looking up at the moon. Everything was still. You could almost see how the glow stood out on top of the surface of the moon. The surface itself was dark, the light like a reflection from some strange headlight-like thing deep in space, the sun from where you couldn't see it, as everybody knows, though not too many people waste their time pondering over it. "*The wat'ry star*," Shakespeare called it, as if he were the first astronaut, claiming it as a part of his world.

I wanted a simple life, I guess. That was all I wanted. Like one of those old Japanese guys who lives in a simple little shack with some Buddha statues inside, who can tell you wise things if you go and ask him, but who generally keeps pretty quiet. Somewhere up in the mountains, or someplace deep in the woods or by a far away lake. I wanted to be a teacher.

I came out from the bare woods by the tennis courts. The dark athletic fields lay beyond a stand of white pine in even rows. Only way far up toward the gym complex could you see the green of the grass underneath the light.

Somewhere beyond the woods, tucked gently into the folds of the land below the rising profile of the Holyoke Range, lay my family's old house, the house of my childhood. It was a small split-level with a brief uphill driveway and White Birch trees my tall father had planted on either side. There had been a lot of farmland back then, tobacco leaves hanging in the long dark barns of the humid flats of the valley, fruit and vegetable stands by the sides of the road with bushels of apples and ears of corn. I remember that safe feeling of being strapped into a toddler seat in the back of the blue Volvo station wagon, looking at my mom's pretty auburny dark brown hair, the warm-smelling fields going by in the summer, lit by sun, hearing the murmurings of daylight as I went to sleep, earlier than anyone else.

We'd go past the old house when we came back to visit in the summertime to see the Gregorians. Each year it seemed a little smaller, a little more closed, a little more private, as if the closer you came the farther away something went. The bushes and the woods had grown up all around, leaving it little like I remembered as a kid who passed freely between the three clean yards of ours and the neighbors.

The grass was stiff under my steps. I walked back toward the dorms.

CHAPTER TWO

Bob O'Donnell hitchhiked out from home. He called me—I was listening to *Bad Moon Rising*—and I drove down and picked him up at the turnpike exit. The campus party that night was in the Phi Gam house on the road coming into town. It was Good Friday. Sunday morning I would be taking the bus out to my grandparents for Easter dinner. The night was warm, a string of car headlamps floating in up the long hill from Northampton. We came up the stairs to the second floor. I saw her on the landing, standing against the wall, looking back at me like she had been waiting for me.

"Hello, Princess," I said, stepping up to her.

She smiled at me gracefully, as if she were hiding something. She looked up at my hair.

"Yeah, I know it's messed up. I can never get a good haircut around here."

She looked up at, as if wanting to smooth back the hair across my forehead. "Just let it grow out a bit," she said, studying my head.

I introduced her to Bob, and we went downstairs to the dance floor. We took turns dancing with her. I went in circles around the room as Bob danced with her. I was a bit drunk and feeling pretty happy.

We went through the door down the dark narrow stairs to the basement, and poured ourselves beer in cups from the little black tube that came from the metal keg. Bob went off to find the bathroom. We were alone in the darkness of the room, sitting on a couch.

"My brother was out visiting from Boston earlier this year. He was looking through the face book. I showed him your picture."

"What?"

"He said girls from the school you went to like to fuck." I held the cup in my lap.

She did not say anything and smiled, her hands poised on her lap.

"Tell me about your brother," she said.

"Oh, he's a handsome guy. Chicks dig him. He's nice to me. We grew up together. When I was a kid he'd pour water on my mattress to make it look like I was a bed-wetter." She laughed, getting both sides of it. I looked over at her and smiled. She looked into my eyes, her hands poised on her lap. "He thinks I have a Christ Complex." We both laughed.

The night became a bit of a blur. The three of us were outside on a side porch underneath a string of white Christmas lights.

Later on I stepped out down the front steps to look up at the stars. I felt clear-headed again. My view over the front yard of the house was eclipsed by the figure of Big Mack coming toward me like a Roman soldier. He had been a hall-mate of mine on Fourth Floor James freshman year. He was the tallest guy in the class, built for something in between football and baseball not necessarily involving coordination so much as bluffing and a giant's oversized self-confidence, so big there was a sort of hollow space in the middle of his chest. He spent summers as a paramedic in the outer boroughs of New York. He had talked his way into being a part of campus security, something no one else had thought of. His position allowed him to be buds with the town cops. Personally, I liked the guy and thought he played his role with a dry sort of humor. He was my friend, a Falstaff jealously guarding his rights to sins of righteousness, where I was perfectly happy with my own and didn't interfere with him, or anyone else for that matter.

"Tarnowski, what are you doing?" his voice boomed over me, his arms folded across his chest.

"Oh, not much. Hangin' out."

I looked up at Mack's face, a fine lightly aromatic layer of sweat on it. I couldn't help smiling.

"I'm takin' you in," Mack said, grasping the collar of my dungaree jacket in his big paw and stepping forward toward the passenger side of the waiting cruiser, pulling me along with him. He had left the motor running, the sound of the police scanner buzzing and popping.

"But I have a friend in town. I have to show him around."

"Come on, I'll give you a ride in the squad car. He'll be fine without you."

"No. There's this girl."

"You're resisting arrest."

I found myself in the car. I was going to jump out again, but moving felt difficult. The whole point of getting in the car was that I was going to escape. I looked out the window at the white portico of the house as the car beneath me began to roll. The traffic light was green at the corner.

I took Bob for lunch in the dining hall, and he gave me the report as we ate our cheeseburgers and fries with soda. "I danced like an idiot," I said.

"It worked," Bob said. They had wondered where I had disappeared to, and when he suggested they go outside to look for me, she told him that he just wanted to get her outside so he could kiss her.

Bob was going out to Boston to visit his sister. I walked him to Main Street. We stood together across the street from Emily Dickinson's brother's house in the shade. A small pickup truck stopped, and I gave him a bear hug, a Russian kiss on both cheeks, and he turned with his soccer duffel bag toward the truck. I felt pretty good.

I went for a walk down toward the playing fields. I came up from the freshly mown soccer fields, passing through some tall grass. The sun was on me, and I remembered walking through the fields above our house. I came upon two girls on their stomachs sunning themselves on towels in the distance, and I felt the feeling that I had seeing deer. They both lay propped up on their elbows, talking about something confidentially, heads turned to one another. I could not see them clearly, without my contacts in, passing within twenty yards of them. They weren't wearing bikinis, just sort of normal clothes, just feeling good like I was to be out in the sun. The further one, there was something about her, her manner confident and relaxed, aware of her own intelligence. It seemed they stopped talking, turning to look over as I walked by self-consciously. I felt them watching me, but in my vision they were blurred just enough. I pretended not to see them and kept on walking. Yes, she did look like her, I thought and then I felt sort of stupid.

There was a party at the Charles Drew House that night. The African-American students who lived there didn't throw a lot of parties, so it was something different. I put on the shiny baggy gym pants I found at the second-hand shop in Northampton, old basketball warm-ups from the golden age of America, putting on a jacket over my shirt. It was a small place, and you knew pretty much everyone there anyway. I was standing by the piano when I saw her come in with two girls.

She came forward. "Hi, how are you feeling today?" She looked away for a moment.

I smiled. "Oh, I'm fine," I shrugged. I looked into her eyes. "I was a bit drunk last night."

"You kept calling me by that p-word," she announced.

"P-word. What's that?"

"You don't remember?"

"No."

"You were calling me Princess."

"That's funny." I thought for a moment, just now remembering it, sort of.

She went away and talked with her friends. Then she put her coat on, gathering her girlfriends and heading toward the door.

She tossed her head back slightly as if to glance at me, to check on me to make sure I was coming. She stepped out through the door and I waited a moment then moved to follow.

I lagged behind them for the two short blocks to the bottom of the hill. They walked briskly along the sidewalk, talking calmly back and forth from what I could tell. I walked at my own pace up the middle of the quiet street and it was a calm deep black starry night out. I would catch them going up the hill. I got to the pathway below the portico of the house easily before them by taking the shortcut across the sloping lawn, Emily Dickinson's brother's house off to the right beyond a stand of pines.

"Hi," I said, as she came up alongside me. She was smiling to herself about something, looking forward. She let herself be stripped off from the company of her two girlfriends without saying as much. We walked across the darkened grass, our shoulders and arms almost touching.

I opened the door for her. Her friends had waited for her, and they were silent as I held the door. I went inside after them.

A beautiful high-breasted black girl named Melody grabbed me and took me out on the dance floor. The Princess stood by herself watching me, waiting. I looked over at her and she turned away so I could look at her. There was just something you wanted to help about her, that made me feel all soft inside and care for her and about everything she did. I swallowed, called upon as when I first saw her.

I thanked Melody and excused myself with a sideways step and then slipping backwards between two couples dancing. It wasn't the only time we had come close. She'd come up to me in the dining hall once when she'd learned I liked Kerouac. She wanted to drive across country. She wanted to know my thoughts on Jack Kerouac. Maybe I should come along.

The Princess pulled herself forward from leaning back against a doorframe. Then we danced. She looked up at me.

The party died out. The dance floor thinned. The music slowed. The lights seemed too bright. We left together into the warm quiet night, walking downhill through the town.

"Would you like to hold my hand," she asked, as if her thoughts were audible, holding her hand out.

"Yes."

We held hands, walking down the path, the town lit gently before us, silent in the night.

"Do you like holding my hand?" she asked.

"I do."

"Where are you from?"

"I'm from a small town in the middle of New York State where my Dad teaches. Have you heard of Hamilton? He used to teach at UMass a long time ago. We used to live here, 'til I was three."

She was prevented by something from looking over at me at the moment.

"Well, it's out in the country. Cornfields, cows, hawks, snowdrifts, a lot of woods. Good thing the college is there."

"Did you grow up on a farm?"

"No," I said, drawing it out. "We built the first modern house in the whole area. Lots of windows. There were a lot of farms around us because we lived up a country road. The school bus picked up all the farm kids on our side of the valley. Chet the bus driver had a toupee on underneath his John Deere cap."

"Did you have any animals?"

"We didn't have any animals, just dogs and cats. We had a duckling, but one day he flew off in a huff and never came back."

"We had a German Shepherd," she said proudly as we walked past a fountain. The ground rose again and the town was still and quiet.

"Oh, I like German Shepherds. Did you walk him?"

"No, I was too little then."

"They get big."

"We would take him in the park."

"The park?"

"Central Park."

"Oh, right. I've heard of that. Duh-uh, do you live near there?"

"Yes."

"Our Corgi would sit at the end of the driveway and chase the manure spreaders going by."

She laughed.

"Did you ever have a cat?" I asked.

"No, I'm allergic to cats."

"Oh, I'm sorry. We had lots of cats."

We passed in underneath the awnings of the low brick shops just down from the town hall.

There were narrow windows on the turret of the town hall. "My brother and I when we lived here, we used to pretend there were archers shooting arrows out of those windows." Then we turned the corner and walked along the quiet street and then onto the Common. She had long strides, her high frame light over the ground, proud as a bird of prey watching from a tree. We followed a row of saplings just coming into bud.

"Are your feet getting wet?"

"No, they're okay."

We were getting close to the college-end of the long common. I had to tie my sneaker. When I bent down I saw shiny pieces of glass imbedded carefully into the ground beneath the grass.

"Do you see that? The ground is shining."

"Yes."

I looked up at her, kneeling still.

"So many people don't notice the world around them," she said.

"Exactly." I stood up and looked at her. "Sometimes you see something no one else sees."

We looked at each other for a moment as we faced one another.

"Come on, I know a shortcut."

"You know a shortcut, huh?"

"Yes, I do."

We went up the grass slope of the Common, then across the street, and under the giant Sycamores in front of the PsiU House, their mottled white bark gleaming like moontrees.

We passed between two fraternity houses crossed the quiet side street and down a driveway. Below the drive downhill there was a small lot beyond which stood an old garage, large and low and vacant.

She stopped, walking a few steps over to the wall, then turning to face me, throwing her head back slightly. I stepped up to her. It was very quiet. We were alone, far from anyone.

"I hate you," she said.

"Oh, you hate me, huh."

I found myself facing her. The space between us, different now, was shorter. I looked into her eyes in the darkness. She stood tall. I looked down the whole length of her, then back up into her eyes. She looked back at me without blinking. She threw her head back slightly, and leaned back against the wall of the garage. Before we had been side by side, which was very nice. I stood and looked into her eyes.

Then she leaned back upright from the wall and turned. I turned and stepped forward so that we were side by side again. I felt a little bit sad all of a sudden. Or happy, I couldn't tell. Or just simply very much alive. Yes. That inextricable mixture of things.

We walked along up a narrow side street to the party. We went down to the taproom for a beer, sharing a cup, then upstairs to the dance floor, a long room with hardwood floors and an empty fireplace, a bare institutional light fixture half-forgotten here and there burning too brightly. The sounds faded into the dark passageways. We stood along the wall.

"Did you want to catch up with your friends?"

A look came over her face.

"Don't you want to be with me?" she said, her eyes flashing a quick look at me as she came away from the wall.

"Of course I do," I said, following her direction. "I was just making sure you were happy."

She did not look at me.

"Yes, I want to be with you." I looked at her, feeling I had screwed things up.

"Yes, yes, yes. Yes," I said.

She moved forward quickly so that I was behind her. I reached up to push the door open for her, and we walked across the yard. The traffic had died out. The stars had gathered into constellations.

"Why is it that no one has any confidence here?" she said suddenly. She stopped as she said it, angry with me. We were under a street lamp. "God, I hate that. It makes everything so difficult."

"I'm sorry. I didn't mean it like that." We walked again.

She was silent. She changed her pace. I adjusted, and then tentatively at first we were walking together again, though not quite as mallard couples in a stream, the male proudly behind, watching everything. There were things I did not know of a practical nature, things you're supposed to learn to make your life and everyone else's a little bit smoother. I felt quietly reminded that the things I did not know might cause me a lot of unnecessary and unwarranted personal sorrow and be unfair as life is unfair, to the sweet, the kind, the gentle, the thoughtful, the meek and the mournful. And maybe such things are necessary to suffer. And then we were back walking together.

"We could walk down past the bars and when the UMass guys come out to say things to me I'll tell them off," she said, returning, a smile coming. "It's fun," she said, privately, and I felt good again, her audience.

"Okay. A walk sounds nice."

We walked back to the campus. It was nice to have someone to walk with, and we didn't need to say anything.

We came to the dining hall. We climbed the steps to the dorm rooms upstairs.

"Wait outside for a moment. I've got to pick things up," she said.

So I waited outside, looking over the balcony. She came back up the hall with a rug.

"Here," she said. "Help me shake out the rug."

"Sure." We flopped the rug over the railing, shaking it out. I pretended to drop the rug.

"Can I come in now?"

She turned without saying anything.

"I'll carry the rug," I said, and she turned and handed it over to me. Then we went to her room.

She sat on her bed, which was up against the wall, just inside the door. The room was small and narrow, a few framed pictures on her neatly kept desk, a poster black and white photograph of a classic *Bugatti* on the wall above her bed. It was the same room we all lived in as freshman, and she seemed not to bother with it too much as she sat down on the little metal-framed bed. I sat down on her bed next to her, our sides not quite touching. I looked around the room.

"You don't seem to like me very much."

"I thought about you all day," I said, quietly, from deep inside, hoarse.

She looked at me, pausing to think about something for a moment.

"You should have a big 'Aw, Shucks' sign hanging around your neck," she said in a bright voice, pleased with something. "Shucks," she said in a country voice.

"That's funny," I said. It was.

"No, you really should."

I shrugged, pressing my lips together, rubbing one palm across the other. I felt like laughing, but I was touched by it too, equal parts that rubbed pleasantly against each other.

She studied me for a moment. Then she leaned back, so I leaned back, stretching myself out. She looked forward now, like she was about to conduct a science experiment.

I looked down at my shiny gym pants.

"I didn't know what the hell to wear tonight. I got these at a thrift shop in Noho. I dunno. They're different. Do you ever go to Northampton?"

"Do you like back rubs?"

"Sure."

"Then you can give me a back rub."

"Oh, I see how it works."

"Yes."

I sat up, letting her put her legs behind me. She lay down with her head across her folded arms. I rubbed her back, up to the base of her neck and along her shoulders. I fumbled with her bra, and then she helped me with it. "The one time this happens and I have a zit on my back," she said. Then she turned over and looked up at me. I looked down at her.

Then our lips met. We kissed and I kissed her with all my happiness.

I kissed her slowly, taking breaths with her lips, and then she took my lip. A warm film of blood came from my lip. She held my lip with her teeth.

I kissed her now along the line of her chin, rubbing my chin against hers and moving down from her underneath her chin, slowly, along the base of her neck, unbuttoning the blouse underneath her sweater. Then the perfectly shaped warm budding sweetness was on my lips.

My mouth met hers in a blinding flash of light, reorienting my world, suddenly changing up and down and sideways, north and south. The connection grew everywhere my mouth, my jaw, my face went, like the sparks and flashes that happen when you rub your eyelids when your eyes are closed. Everywhere and within, the sweet ache of a polarity finally met, and all things flowed in and out of me and I was with her at the center of the universe. And I would never be the same, but awakened, called to life.

I kissed her, moving slowly downward, over her belly to her waist. She pulled me back up to her. She turned the lights back on and looked up at me, studying my face. "Would you rub my back some more?"

"Sure. This bone is connected to the arm bone. This bone's connected to the neck bone..."

"You like bones, don't you?'"

"Don't analyze me," I said, softly and gently, continuing the song.

"I wasn't analyzing you," she said somewhat sharply.

"Oh, okay." I felt stupid for breaking the spell. I hadn't meant to. I had just meant to give her all of myself.

Then we sat up and talked again, just little things back and forth, a bit awkwardly, trying to figure out what should happen next. And then I said I had to get going. It was four in the morning by now. "I've got an early bus out in the morning."

I hugged her, holding her tight. I stepped back, kissed her again and walked up the hall. She was leaning silently on the doorway when I looked back.

I found myself outside, under the stars. It was colder now and I walked quickly down the hill. I came in through the bare cold light of the bathroom to the silent darkness of the still hallway. Bob and Peter were away for Passover. Spike had gone down to Connecticut to his folks for Easter. I went upstairs and had a beer with my friend Burt, who was part of a Christian room group and grinned a lot and blinked his eyes. And again, there were things I did not know, the technical things about how to act once you feel a certain way. I was entirely new to feeling all my dreams having come true. I didn't know you had to say it all out loud. In fact, that seemed contrary to my reasoning. So I had a beautiful secret with me, that only I knew, and to tell you the truth, it had not been ruined, not at all, but only made a little sweeter, as was only proper. I bit my lip softly, and felt the place she had touched.

I woke up very early with the alarm clock at the first light of Easter morning with a good amount of energy. I showered quickly, dressed neatly in clean chinos and an oxford and took the parcels of flowers under my arm. A light mist, transparent in the early sunlight, hung above the hill. I felt the droplets of dew on my face. I thought of how she would be sleeping still. The world was new in the light, and it felt wonderful to be up early.

The bus pulled into Springfield. There was no bus Westward along the Massachusetts Turnpike for more than two hours. They had not bothered to tell me at the bus company counter when I bought the ticket. So I sat alone on the silent dock platform, warming myself in the sun. I was thinking about the girl and didn't want to call anyone. I could just trust fate now, I thought.

The bus to Lee rolled up into its slot finally. When we got there the door opened and I climbed down into the cool sunlight, crossed the street and called my grandparents from the phone outside the drug store. I waited for my aunt to arrive on a park bench on the sunny side of the street by the town hall. I had made a bit of a mess of it.

My aunt—it turned out she had driven all the way out to Amherst to look for me anyway-- took me across town past the paper mill along the stream toward the school where she taught. We were good friends from my summer visits. Some girlfriends of hers, fellow high school teachers, were having a little wine and cheese get-together. I followed my aunt up to the brown-painted house and we went out on a small deck of pressure-treated wood. A woman, in a tinselly blue sweater, her cheeks flushed, her eyes moist, unsteady, looked at me as she held her dark blue ceramic wine goblet. "I think Jamie's kinda' cute," she said, almost hiccupping. She swayed toward a plate of cheese and fruit, selecting a cube of honeydew melon with her fingers, holding it a moment before bringing it up to her face. She shrugged, crinkled up her nose, and peeked at me as she took another sip of wine. I turned and looked over the yellowy grass of the backyard. I thought about the girl, pretending she was standing next to me.

We came back through the small town tucked in amongst the hills. The road rose out of town. We came past the golf course. The homes were bigger, four in a row with stables, colonial and painted white at the turn off. We went up the hill, passing some more regular kinds of houses with regular yards. We went over the top of the hill, into the woods, past a barn, and then the small brick duplex ranch house on the left.

"Your grandfather used to take your mother and I driving around Boston. He showed us the bums lying out on the sidewalks and he'd say, 'you see that guy? He used to be a doctor. That guy was a banker. Then the bottle got 'em,'" my aunt said self-consciously.

"Oh, man."

We came in through the warm hallway and I said my greetings, feeling half like my dad and half guilty for screwing everything up.

My grandfather, a chef, carved the turkey. I helped my grandmother up from the couch where she watched television behind a standing tray. She stood stiffly. "Thank you, Darlin,' she said turning to smile at me once she was on her feet.

"I fell in with evil companions..." I said, reciting, leaning down to her.

"And had a good time," she said, smiling again, completing one of her expressions. We all sat down for Easter dinner. I cut off a piece of white meat and put it in my mouth. I looked over my plate. Evenly mashed potatoes, thick gravy, bright green peas, and cranberry sauce, warm puffy rolls, chilled butter to cut off in little squares.

I helped with the dishes. I was thinking I could be getting back to the bus station.

"Why don't you stay the night," my grandfather said. "Jamie," he added, as if remembering my name. "I'll drive you back in the morning."

"Yeah, okay. Sure." I felt bad about coming late.

"You can stay in the red room." This was the room with a fold-out couch bed my brother and I always slept on when we came for Christmas. The room had red carpet and a commemorative plaque on the walls for my grandmother's years as a waitress, a golden statue of a chef from the university where Papa had worked. My grandfather had a new stereo system, turntable, tape deck, the whole bit. I put the dishtowel down and looked out of the kitchen into the living room. The television commanded the room from a cabinet below an oil painting of the surf rolling in with whitecaps, the moonlight making the waves transparent where they were about to roll over. The sliding door to the screened-in stained redwood porch led to the laundry room. My aunt came back in with her Cocker Spaniel and said a round of good nights.

The short man sat down at the dining room table after washing himself, his shirt open, a white tee-shirt underneath. He had been in the bathroom for a good twenty minutes. There was something boyish about him now in the hunch of his neck. I sat down with him. We had a cup of coffee. He lit a cigarette.

"I saw an Edward G. Robinson film once," he said. "This guy goes back to his college reunion. He's a bum but he dresses up in a tuxedo and acts like he's a big shot." My grandfather looked over at me, snorting up something deep within the dark hairs of his nose, a line of blue smoke rising from his cigarette as he held it by the ashtray. There was a dark stain at the corner of his mouth. "Everyone's a lawyer or a doctor, and in the end he tears off his jacket and says, 'I'm a bum. I'm nothing but a damn bum,' he says."

"Sounds like a good movie."

"Quite touching," Papa said, serious, quieter, raising his chin. He looked down at the cigarette cupped in his hand, then looked over his shoulder back over at the open door to the bedroom where Nana was asleep. The radio was blaring from within beyond the foot of the bed.

He looked down as he finished his cigarette, snuffing it out in the pewter ashtray.

My grandfather went to bed, walking stiffly off to the bedroom in his boxer shorts. I didn't feel like looking through the President Kennedy picture book on the small shelf next to the linen closet. There were some *Readers Digest* books bound over by the door. I put my coat on and let myself out, closing the metal storm door gently, the brick showing through the white paint underneath the overhead outdoor light.

I walked across the small yard, past the cement birdbath under the spindly pines. The road was very quiet. I looked back at the house in the small clearing in the tall trees lining the edge of the road. It felt good to be out in the woods, as if I were to find there the things that people thought of.

I walked up the road in the darkness, and the night sky had never been blacker, and the stars never as brilliant, the sound of the tree frogs in the swamp on the lowest part of the stretch of the narrow road, the sound of the earth thawing. There was wind brushing the pines above making whooshing sounds, full of song. I had met her at last and she was my secret.

I stood for a long while in the pitch black of the road thinking of the night before and how my instincts had proven right and my dreams had come true. I had been very patient, but I had known something from first seeing her. I could almost feel her hand when I put my hand on the desktop before me. She was quiet, drawn inward. It was gravitational pull. And yet, why was I alone now? It was the perfect night to be with her.

The day was a sign of my purity, and I was pleased with the way it had gone. I turned finally and walked back toward the distant glow above the woods beyond the thicket above the swamp. I crossed the yard, pulled the storm door open, put my hand gently on the knob and opened the green front door.

As I lay awake, waiting to fall asleep, maybe I thought of how love is long-suffering, how it endures all. Only after one was finally a man would an acorn drop and fall to the ground to be embraced, and then to live, the song of the wind seemed to say to me as I fell toward sleep. Only then, the finest hour, a whole season coming to a single moment, or else there wouldn't be a planet in the middle of deep space with the wind blowing its song and its poetry and its time.

Papa drove me back in the morning. I remembered how he took me and my brother to the shore where we walked along the rocks. I felt something rising in my chest as we climbed the hills of the Mass Pike, the sun above the beautifully God-created undulating conifer-covered mountains, perfect hills laid one after another, and each one a perfect place for a town, for a life, and especially coming up the last hill into town, the college suddenly before us at the crossroads, the sun quietly across the smooth sloping lawn before the old library.

We went to a small coffee house overlooking the Common two doors from Hastings, the newspaper store that had always been there. It was in one of those old buildings that had always been there and always will be. It was tall like a barn, big enough to hold a theater inside. There was something slightly sagging, or crooked about it, as it settled, like a sail meeting a wind. "Why don't you get a blueberry muffin," Eddie White said as we looked over the glass below the counter. We sat there at the wooden shelf looking over the street, not saying anything. I broke my blueberry muffin, buttered it and brought a piece of it to my mouth. I wanted to tell him about girls I'd met, but I felt anxious, wanting to move on to my life and maybe he felt that and understood.

We walked outside to my grandfather's *Camry*. I leaned down and hugged him. He looked up at me for a moment through his glasses, a faint far off smile deep in the thickness of his face, accepting my attempt to say what there was to say. Being Irish from his side I felt sentimental with a brash sort of youthfulness, loved him with honesty. He'd had handsome dark hair, just like my brother's in the one picture I'd ever seen of him as a young man.

"Come out to a football game next fall," I called to him as he opened the car door and climbed stiffly in, lifting his foot up, pulling the door shut. There were stories of him and cars.

I watched him pull out from the parking space and then turn around on the wide side street that cut the Common in half. Then the car turned onto Route Nine. I walked up the grassy hill toward the Chapel.

That afternoon I called her and set up a date. At eight o'clock I went by her room. The televisions were on in the rooms along the hallway, each door open with the excitement of basketball. She stopped outside one of the doors, looking in at the television. The short pretty redhead girl in the room turned back to her, as if they had already spoken about something.

We went for a walk up past the library and across the quad to the War Memorial. We sat down on one of the granite benches, laid out in a ring like tombs of buried knights.

"Do you like being alone?"

"I guess I can stand it. It's not so bad when you're thinking about something."

"What do you think about?"

"Oh, you'll probably laugh," I said, turning to her. "Poems I've read. People. Books. How you talk about life."

"Maybe that's not always a good thing to do, to think, all by yourself."

"I know. It just ends up that way."

"But you always look so sad."

I sunk my head down.

"I didn't think anyone would notice. I didn't think anyone really cared around here. No one ever asks me anything, like, 'how are you doing.' They just assume everything is going well because everyone else here is doing so well and dandy."

"What's wrong?"

I shrugged, my hands in the pockets of my Levi's jacket. Our legs were touching, at the knee.

"There's so much to learn about words and about people and their feelings. Where do you start?"

"But why are you so sad?"

"Oh, it just comes with the territory, I guess, because life is sad sometimes. It's beautiful and no one pays any attention to it."

"You shouldn't think too much. You're smart. There are a lot of things you could be doing with yourself."

I moved my knee away, afraid I had imposed it on her, but she moved her hand down and pulled my knee back to hers. She turned and faced me, looking into my eyes.

"I want to give it my all, you know."

"That just makes you lonely and unresponsive," she said quietly.

I leaned back and looked up at the moon. It had climbed up above the gymnasium. "All the guys who've been up there, when they come back here they understand. When you're up on the moon, you're a long way away and you look back and see this blue round thing we live on, makes you believe you're here for a reason," I said.

"But you can overshoot the moon and just keep on going right out into space, never to come back."

I laughed. "Yeah. I saw a movie like that once. The computer went bad on them. He wanted to take control of everything."

We sat there a little while longer. I buttoned up my jacket. "Are you cold?" She nodded.

"Let's go back then."

We passed the library, a bank of lit windows underneath brick cellblock through the pine trees.

"Do you know the woman who works at the front desk of the library at night? She's in our class. Dark hair, tall, athletic? All the guys in my class think she's beautiful, but I listen to her voice when she comes on the p.a. system to say the library is closing in ten minutes... and it just sounds sort of cold and harsh to me. I wouldn't want her talking to my children that way." It sort of surprised me that I was talking about Eva Horner this way. "Maybe that's just how some people do things."

I looked down at the dark glistening grass.

She leaned up against me with her shoulder, bumping me unexpectedly.

"You are one of the few guys around here I find sexually attractive," she said.

"Oh, okay." The leg cuffs of my jeans were wet. The grass was making me think of something far back somewhere.

We went back to her room. I sat down on the chair at her desk across from her bed.

"Why can't you come sit next to me?" she said from the bed, where she was sitting, leaning back against the wall.

"Oh, okay. I'd like that. Thanks." I sat down next to her, and leaned back.

"Don't thank me."

"Okay."

We were sitting close together now so that the sides of our legs were touching. It was comfortable again, back to the way it was at first.

"My mom, she always regretted us leaving Amherst. When my dad left UMass he was going to help start up this woman's college. But then there was a lot of politics. The whole thing got absorbed by the brother school and my dad lost his tenure."

I looked up at her just to make sure I wasn't boring her, going on too long. "Well, my Mom, she had all this anxiety. She'd go off on my dad a lot, yelling at him, 'you're a failure, you're a failure.' This gentle guy who was always working, correcting papers, drawing up lesson plans, all the care he put it into over all the years. He'd be up 'til midnight working on something in his chair every night."

"What happened?"

"One summer she went to the hospital, and stayed for... I don't know, a month or so, I guess. We ate a lot of hamburgers that summer. My brother and I would be watching *Superman* and Dad would be cooking out on the grill in the back yard. After dinner we would drive into Utica to see Mom in the hospital. We'd visit, then on the way back we discovered the radio station played the same song list at the same time, so when we turned up the road going home the same song was playing. '*Angie*...' I remember it."

I shrugged.

"We'd go see her and she'd tell us about what it was like being there. There was a woman on her floor who would sing, 'who's afraid of the big bad wolf' to herself. Like she was lost, in the woods or something."

She was looking forward, her lips open slightly.

"Then Mom went to a shrink for a long time. Stuff from her childhood, her father coming home drunk from the restaurants, causing a scene... Being lonely and cooped up in the house didn't help, not having any neighbors around. I don't blame her. Not like it was her fault."

I felt relaxed sitting on the bed, leaning up against the wall. I looked across at her desk, studying the pictures on it.

"They're just two people, and that's all they are. And you'd hope that there would be enough to keep them together. I'm afraid there isn't though, the way the world is sometimes."

I looked over at her, then back across the desk.

"I always thought they loved each other." We were silent for a moment. "But what does a kid know?"

I felt relaxed sitting on the bed, leaning up against the wall. I looked across at her desk, studying the pictures on it. "Why do people have to go through all that? They're just improvising, as best they can, just like everyone else. Just like we are."

She took her lower lip in her teeth. "My father tried to teach me how to drive last summer at the farm," she said quietly, prepared to laugh. "I could never tell where the danger was coming from." She looked over at me into my eyes.

"Yeah, that's what it's like. It's like friends. You love everyone, but maybe that's not always good. You have to be selfish sometimes. Otherwise you end up doing all these things you don't want to do and your heart aches and you get all confused. Doing stupid shit. Because you couldn't listen to yourself and what you wanted to do. Hell, that's hard enough anyway, with all the things that get into your own head."

There was a small night table with a shelf of books. She traced along the row of the tops of the bindings with her index finger. "My mother writes mysteries," she said. She pulled a narrow paperback out.

"That's so cool," I said, leaning sideways as I sat.

She pushed the book back in.

"Let me see."

She turned and looked away.

She took the Calculus book from the top of the nightstand and pulled it on to her lap.

"I have a tutor. One of your friends, I think. Rick. He has red hair." She opened the big hardcover book up and looked down at it.

"Oh, yes. We call him the Captain of Leisure. He has a great loft. Do you like him?"

"He's nice." She said it in a way that reassured me.

She was looking down in her book again, as if she needed help. I felt the urge to take the book from her lap and kiss her. But we were side by side, and I liked that very much.

"Well, it's getting late. I guess I should go," I said. I bit my lip, and it felt fat.

I stood up, and then she stood up before me. We hugged, our bodies close, touching from leg to shoulder, drawn together, so complete, the perfection of company I had never known.

"Hmmmm." A purring sort of sound came from my chest as I exhaled, holding her there in my arms.

And I heard from her the same sound of what my body was feeling, as she was murmuring 'hmmmm," as well, so that hers seemed to be the sound coming from me. Something inside both of us, perfectly in tune.

"I'll see you later," I said softly, pulling back. I had the feeling of knowing something with certainty in my heart, again with a kind of sweet-tasting sadness that made me feel clean and good, my hair standing on end.

"Bye," she said, her voice rising slightly, looking up at me, studying my departure in the blue sea of her eyes.

Then I turned and left, walking down the hall. I stopped at the end of the hallway and looked back. She was in the doorway still, as if she were watching a child do something he was going to do. "Good night," I said, smiling, and walked away down the stairs, all my sorrows about me like a cloak.

My roommates were up when I came in, taking Karate kicks at an old mattress leaning up against the wall by the bathroom door. I'd told them before where I was going.

"How did it go?" Peter asked, and the three of them looked at me, as if anyone needed to say anything.

"We had a nice talk," I said.

"Good. Why aren't you still over there?"

"Oh, I don't know... don't want to move too fast."

"You don't want to move too slow, either."

I thought about it as I went to bed. A strange feeling I didn't understand came over me, and I lay there on the thin mattress alone, looking up at the ceiling, the light out, the vinyl shade pulled down.

Walking across the grass with her I felt it, maybe for the first time. There was this shell we all carry around, made up of things like cowardice, fear, being passive and agreeable, all those things which make you not say how you really feel. Inside the shell there was a normal kind wise person. But the shell keeps you from things. The shell was not a problem around the people you cared about, people like my mom, my dad, my brother. It didn't matter then. But the shell could control how you acted, and it seemed you had to reach out to find a steady way to make yourself feel comfortable to say what you wanted to say.

And yet I felt the shell wasn't there when I was next to her. I didn't need to be anyone but myself when I was with her. We were comfortable around each other. We could talk about anything, without any lies. And the things we did together went deep inside of me.

It was like when you saw someone beautiful and wanted very much for her to notice you as you were doing whatever you really were doing, and I felt that awesome and simple joy that she had noticed me and that we had connected. And that was all I needed out of life.

And at the same time, her face was so beautiful, a joy to me, that I felt some great awful beatific vision dawning across my consciousness that life is not about happy things, but about what we all might share, all the things that comprised me, my worries, my sadnesses, my illnesses, my poverty, my foolishness, my fears and faults and all things that made me just want to live a simple life amongst other poor and worried tender people like myself.

The next night I went looking for her in her dorm room. "She just left," the short redhead told me, not quite looking at me, confident of her own unique feminine powers. "She's going up to the bus stop." She looked past me before I turned to leave.

I walked briskly toward the old library. I saw her up ahead. A dungaree jacket covered her shoulders. I jogged up beside her. She kept her own pace.

"Hey," I said.

"Oh," she said. "Hi,' she said, looking forward still then with her chin up. She put her hands in the side pockets of her jacket.

The bus turned in off the main road, the lights swinging across the space before us, the land sloping down from the Octagon. The bus turned again, the engine exhaling as it came too fast toward us, then lurching to a quick stop. Gas released with a pop, and the lights inside above the driver came on, the doors opening. The bus rumbled in its hindquarters. I tried to think of something to say quickly just then, a question, maybe.

"I'm going to see a friend over at Hampshire," she announced in a high tone, her chin raised, not looking over at me. She took a step forward to the bus, calculating the right moment to board. She stood still for a moment.

"I need to do some reading for Shakespeare," I said, my foot on the base of the granite steps of the old library. A tree was lit in the distance by a solitary street lamp. I tried to say something again. A wave of cold came up from the dark pavement.

"Bye," she said, nonchalantly, mounting the first step, her hair lit by the cold colorless light of the cab of the bus.

I stood there about to say something. The driver stared forward. The door closed. I watched her pass in steps through the front to a seat on the far side of the bus. The stiff blue-detailed interior lit by the fluorescent tubes hung in space before me for a moment, then lurched into motion, pulling her away, as she looked down and out the far window, privately expectant of her trip. Then the back of the bus pulled away, turning left onto the road with a swing pulling its own gravity.

I walked slowly and numbly up to the library. The pine needles were all quiet under the yew bushes out front. There wasn't anyone on the quad. I went inside and sat down on the second floor, the little playbook in front of me. I read a little while, and then I put my chin down in my arms, then blocking the lights out, no one on the floor except me.

The next Saturday night the campus was ready for the Beach Party at Chi Phi, across the street from the music building. I saw her in the dining hall standing in the hallway between the two entrances, people about us talking as they passed back in forth between the different dining rooms, East and West. She glanced up at my head without expression.

"Do you like my Beach Party hair cut?" I said, rubbing the back of my head where the guy had cut it close.

"It's short," she said, curtly, looking off at the crowd.

"Are you going tonight?"

"Yes," she said.

Later on, I went to the party. A plastic palm tree cut out stood on a drift of a sand dune in a corner of the hallway. People passed it with slightly wobbling quickness, sunglasses propped up on their heads. We went out on the dance floor. She looked away, off beyond my shoulder. The band played loud, intonation clashing, rhythm churning, vocals blurred, the drums drowning. Her face tightened further. "Let's go sit down," I shouted at her finally.

We sat down on a couch back in the front hall sheltered away from the music. We both were silent. I put my arm out on the armrest. I wasn't going to protest.

"I like your pants," I said softly, feeling that she was about to say something, gathering up her breath for it, just waiting for the right moment. Her pants were woven, with a hippie-sort of stripe about them. It was an obvious thing to say, like tossing a beach ball in a high arc to a child.

"You know," she said, raising her voice above the level of conversation, "I'm sorry, but it's chemistry."

I looked back at her, her arms extended to her knees, her chin down.

"Yes, it is chemistry," I said, and my voice was deep, peaceful.

I stood up.

"Good night," I said evenly. I turned and left her sitting with the same expression. I felt lighter, and freer, upright as I moved amongst the football players, the preppies, the smokers who all belonged with each other.

Later I saw her standing. I felt her through the crowd. I got a cigarette from a very Nordic blond fancy senior girl with the tanned slenderness of Waspy old ladies who play too much tennis, her gaze forward, the angle of her chin, the broadness of the back of her jaw acknowledging herself as a paragon of something, something I didn't want. Nothing against her, she was kind enough to me, just that she had a stick of some sort way up her ass, her general attitude. I had a beer in my hand, feeling rebellious. The Princess stood at a distance, but I turned from her carefully each time, pretending something in another direction was more important.

As I lay down in bed that night back in my room before sleep I thought about her. I sort of laughed about how she had just been with me as if it was good she was being that way with me, almost like we had agreed on how to act with each other.

I hugged my pillow in my arms and put my face on it and I said I love you to her.

CHAPTER THREE

The next Saturday night after the Beach Party I set myself up in an all-night study room in Chapin Hall.

By eleven fifteen I had enough. I left my books on the long table below the fluorescent lights and sat down outside on the slate steps. Far across the yard the communal television in the lounge of the dining hall flickered blue white light. *Saturday Night Live*. My heart thumped an extra beat at it. I crossed the yard and walked up to the entryway.

I sat down in an upholstered chair next to a matching couch, my head back, watching the opening monologue of some actor I didn't recognize.

She came in quickly and plopped down on the couch, crossing one leg over the other. She sat there, looking at the screen.

"Hey," I said.

"Hi," she said.

A blond newscaster had climbed up on her knees on the top of a news desk, spanking herself on the bottom.

"It's all about sex," the Princess declared.

She sat for a moment, folding her arms and looking at the television screen.

I looked quickly over at her and back at the screen, my hands on the two arms. "Yeah, it is, I guess."

There was a roll-on deodorant commercial and then the show came back on. She rose, tossing her head back slightly as she looked down at the large console television before her. Then she turned and walked toward the stairs.

I watched her as she climbed the stairs. At the turn onto the landing a slight satisfied smile came to her face, the angle of her head a ballet movement of a look back. As if to catch me looking at her, longing for her, like I knew I was.

I sat in front of the television for a while longer. I sat there, flipping my fingers on the fabric of the outside of the armrest. Now there wasn't anything to do. I stood and walked back across the quadrangle toward Chapin and the vacant upstairs classroom with the long tables to pack it up. Out on the quadrangle beneath the stars again, I looked up at her window. The light was off. I walked away under the trees down the long hill to my room.

The guys were playing *Yahtzee* on a coffee table in the social room. I poked my head up the stairs and looked in on them. There was a blue cloud of cigar smoke and they were yelling "Zatz!" at each other. They weren't drinking anything, just yelling and laughing with the cigars in their mouths. I went back to my room, picked up my electric, turned the amp on low and strummed a few chords and then I went to bed without a word.

Every other Wednesday was Spaghetti Night. I walked down from the library along the path, a mist held up higher in the trees. I came in through the line at the big hall at the end, picking up a tray, silverware from the bins, sliding the tray down along the stainless steel shelf beneath the bright lights. I got to the woman at the entree station.

She reached with tongs into the stainless pan and put a good portion of the noodles on the plate. Then she ladled up some meat sauce on top, a piece of bay leaf sticking out. She handed the plate to me, looking up at me through her thick glasses with a sympathetic look, the smells of basil, oregano, onions and tomato rising above the row of steam tables behind glass.

I didn't see anyone I knew out in the dining room, so I took a smaller round table somewhere in the middle of the room. I didn't mind sitting alone after I had studied. Let the chatter surround you and your thinking picks up again where you left off.

Stanley came out of the line with his tray. I nodded to him.

"What's going on, Beastie?" Stanley said, sitting down, looking around the room.

"How's acting class?"

"Jenny Havermeyer liked that thing I did about the guy outside the graveyard, freaking out." Stanley rolled his head back, his neck up straight, and looked about the room with big eyes shifting back and forth, narrowing them. "He's waiting for a bus and he starts to hear this shit. He's like…" he said in a thick-timbered voice, twitching his head slightly, slipping into his role, "…looking back behind him."

I twirled up a forkful of spaghetti. I looked down at it as it sat on my plate. "Graveyards are good material."

"Yeah, she was digging it. I got a date set up with her."

I thought of how she'd hung around the salad bar once in the fall after I'd cut my hair short. Just a little too long. As if she wanted someone to ask her if she wanted to join him. I looked around, and there wasn't anyone else. But I'd let it pass.

"Any James Dean stories?"

"No. George Stevens liked to shoot everything over and over again, from different angles, and that drove him crazy," I said.

We ate in silence for a little while.

"They were shooting that knife fight scene in *Rebel Without a Cause*, and the other guy nicked him and he started bleeding a little bit, like on his shirt, and the director stopped the filming. And James Dean got all mad."

I looked out across the room. There was a lot of talking going on. A lot of moving faces.

"Maybe that's the only time he could express himself, playing someone else."

Stanley put a big one in his mouth.

"James Dean liked spaghetti. 'Spaghetti boy' the waiters called him, this place he liked to go to in New York City," I said.

"Mmmm," Stanley said, looking up halfway from his plate.

"There were all sort of things he was curious about, things he wanted to understand better."

We ate and I went up past the tall pines to the library. The sky was dark, overcast, no moon. After nine I called the Princess from the black campus phone on the third floor.

"So what are you doing this summer?"

"I'll find a job down in the City."

"Work in some office?"

"Yes, probably. And you?"

"I've got my usual gig at the college grounds keeping crew."

"Get a real life," she said, using an expression in vogue, aloof again after a brief pause, like a bird flown up to perch in the high part of a tree.

"It is a real life," I said from the ground. "You get your own truck with a radio to listen to country music. A tractor. Chain saws, shovels. A shed to hang out in on rainy days with bags of peat moss to sleep on or sit back on and drink coffee. And all sorts of rakes. A lot of rakes. Big iron ones, light metal ones, and of course the classic bamboo model."

She didn't say anything.

"We get to plant trees, too. You can go back years later and say, 'I planted that.'"

"Well have fun with all your rakes this summer."

"Um, did you ever see James Dean in *Giant*?" I said quickly.

"Is he your hero?" she said with an indirect scoff, enunciating the two syllables of the last word.

"Yes, he is."

I thought she would say something. She kept quiet, listening.

"Most people think he was just driving fast, but it wasn't his fault. He was going straight and some other guy didn't see him. He went to a Buddhist monastery two weeks before he died, I read once."

She didn't say anything, but it sounded like she was listening.

"Have a good night," I said, and hung up the phone.

James Dean put up this shell around himself. When he was acting, he broke through that. He revealed parts of himself that he never showed, things he never shared. He wanted to share them, but when do you say such things and to whom do you talk with about them? He acted, became fully alive and human, sharing all that stuff, anger, jealousy, hurt, caring, wanting, all that stuff.

The artist is someone who has a shell, but who seeks a way out. He knows he has a lot inside, and he knows subconsciously that he must train it to come out. He learns a process that works for him. He learns how to protect that.

In a way, actors have it easy. Everyone sees an actor act. Being on stage you can't miss him. But a writer, he's got to do it alone, and all by himself. Something he must use to his advantage somehow.

There was a party the next Saturday night at the boy's wing of her dorm. There was a keg of beer in the bathroom in the wing opposite from hers. I had on this leisure jacket I'd found at a secondhand store, a hideous jungle plaid.

I stood in the hall with a cup of beer in my hand, minding my own business. I did not really expect to her to make an appearance, because she thought these kinds of parties were juvenile and useless, a keg in the boys room, a little bit of predictable music, *Animal House,* Madonna, some disco and the like. I felt comfortable with my odd-ball jacket of middle-class leisure. Too bad the jacket didn't have matching pants. I wondered if the

Princess might show up. I talked to Schaller, who played Yahtzee with the boys, and we drank a few beers.

A friction had recently developed with some underclassmen, stemming from an incident involving a cheer that I had given when the football team won at home. My brother told me about it freshman year. I would stand up toward the end of a game when we were winning and say as I pointed, "Is that not the goal post there." And the people in the stands around me, having been enlisted to do so, would say, "Yes, that is the goal post there." And so it would go, with me pointing out different things, the referee, the thirty yard line, even Coach Meissner himself, until finally I would point over at the home team and say, "is that not the winning team," to which the chorus would respond, and then point over across the field at the humbled visitors, "is that not the losing team," echoed again by the chorus, then back and forth, "winning team, losing team, winning team, losing team." (There was even some talk of my becoming the new Lord Jeff mascot. No thanks. I would have brought out blankets for the other side of the field, which would have been in bad taste, given the real history of Lord Jeffrey Amherst.)

One day that year at the game I heard my cheer being used. "Some kid's giving your cheer, Jamie," the guys I was sitting with said, looking over at me, as if I didn't notice. I didn't really care but it seemed they were asking me to do something about it. So I went down the stands and walked up to the kid, basking in the praise of his peers. I reached my hand out and grabbed the kid's cheeks lightly between my thumb and fingers, squeezing the kid's mouth, so that he now had fish-lips. "That's my cheer," I said to the kid. I don't know what possessed me to do it, other than that I was hungover from staying up too late with a couple of guys who had graduated the year before. I hadn't intended to be violent. Maybe it was the pudginess to the kid's face that made one want to squeeze his face so. I didn't do it hard or anything. I was depressed that day and didn't know about it, or what to do with myself.

It would have ended peaceably but for a loud-mouthed classmate of the pudgy-faced kid. I was about to shrug it off and walk away. He gets on my case, as if it wasn't a private matter between me and the kid who took my cheer. Like it was my cheer. "You couldn't take me in a fight," the loudmouth smug-faced kid said, starting in on me instantly. I wondered where that had come from. Later he came up to a party we, the guys in my suite, were hosting. "You want to step outside and settle this," said the kid, a golfer. "Let's just forget about it. I already apologized to Brennan." I felt stupid about the whole thing.

The kid looked me in the eye like he had a point to make. "We both know who would win," the kid, whose name was Luke, said. I just smiled, as if I was an idiot, letting it all drop passively. The kid finished his beer with a fat trivial air of victory and stalked off into the night, returning downstairs to his own familiar suite and his golf clubs.

It was almost one now. Schaller was leaving and I was ready to go. We turned onto the main hallway leading between the two wings, with the stairs to the left in the middle. I saw her standing, just up the hallway. She was with a girl, a shorter blond of a common American sort of prettiness, who happened to be going out with the kid who said he could beat me in a fight. He was there, talking to them, feeling very important, and had given himself the floor concerning whatever they were discussing. The Princess, prepared to nod or say nothing contrary, studied him directly, apparently interested in what he was going on about.

I walked up the hall toward them. I leaned toward Schaller, pretending not to notice her, as if I was part of an important conversation, about to deliver a good piece of advice, like a trusted lawyer. I turned my brow toward her. We turned and walked down the steps. A feeling of powerlessness seemed to be coming on more and more and I didn't know what to do.

The last day of classes came and then exam week and the turning-in of final papers. I had almost finished up my final paper for Middle Eastern History. In the beginning I had enthusiasm for it, but I could only manage a sloppy job. I had half of it typed. The rest I'd given up on. Fuck it. In the afternoon I walked away from the campus, across the town common. I passed along a line of Norway Maples decked with a spray of light green flowers. I walked down through town along the main strip, past the restaurants and the bars. *Barselotti's*, a neon sign above a big picture window looking out over the sidewalk, had been there since my mother was at UMass. Nobody I knew ever went there. It was a mild overcast day, a uniform of green about every corner of town like a halo.

Behind the counter of the florist's shop stood a wide refrigerator with glass doors slightly fogged by humidity. I looked briefly over the bundles of long-stemmed cut flowers in dark green pots, their colors muted by the water droplets along the glass. A mild man stood behind the counter, a roll of green tissue paper before him. He looked at me without saying anything. I asked him for a dozen white roses.

A low blanket of clouds came in during dinner. I went back to my room and wrote out the last two pages of my paper as neatly as I could, not bothering to type them. I went over to Professor Demetrious's office in Chapin and slipped the paper under the door. The only good part of the paper was that I had put in a line about "the chickens coming home to roost," a phrase the professor was fond of. Dusk had fallen, and the rain came lightly with a fresh pebbly smell and intermittently at first. The rain was on the grass and I thought about the cool flowers in the box.

Tiny fresh leaves were out now on all the trees, blossoms on the dogwoods planted around the buildings, the forsythia out in bright yellow bloom. The rain tapped lightly upon each leaf one by one, fresh and new to the world. I walked past the dining hall. A slight wedge of light came from the side of the blind of her window.

I walked back to my room, getting my things in order to pack. I looked in the mirror, put on the slate blue jacket from one of my father's old suits, picked up the narrow box, took a deep breath and slipped out the bathroom door and down the stairs.

I walked uphill in the rain. The hallway was quiet, with doors closed. I stood in front of her door. I felt she was nearby, hiding.

I walked back to my dorm and packed up my desk, taking the maps and posters down from the wall.

It was getting later. I looked out the back door. It was raining harder down the concrete steps and the drops of rain on the cement below. I took the box under my arm and walked back up the hill to her dorm to her hall, to her door. I saw it was open as I came up to it.

"Hello," I said. I put my shoulder gently to the door and walked in.

She turned and glared at me for a moment, then turned back down to the piles of clothes she was going through, sorting to be packed.

I came in and sat down at the edge of the bed, feeling that somehow she had been tipped off.

"Need any help?"

"No," she said in a loud sharp voice.

"Okay, well here, I brought you something."

"I don't want them." She said each word independently.

"Oh, come on," I said gently.

"No!"

"They're just flowers," I said.

"I don't want them!"

The room felt surprisingly large to me, as if she were down at the end of a long hall. Maybe that was what she felt too so that she had to raise her voice, almost yell at me. I looked down at my arms folded across the top of the long neatly-tied box sitting on my lap.

She picked up a folded sweater from the top of one pile, and put it down on the other, quickly and heavily.

"Are your parents coming to pick you up?"

She was silent.

I sat there.

She turned to me then and took a step forward.

"Give them to your parents," I said quietly.

"No!" she said, her lips flaring, stomping her foot down so as to frighten me.

I stood up. I placed the box of flowers down on the bed. I bit my lip.

"I'm just bringing them to you. That's my job. Flush them down the toilet if you want to. I don't care what you do with them."

She turned away. I looked up for a moment at the *Bugatti* on the wall. One of the longest cars ever made.

I picked up the box of flowers, took it under my arm and turned quietly to the door. She turned to come toward me, gathering her strength to push me but for the flash of uncertainty across her face.

At the door I turned to look at her. A drip of water came down across my brow. My jacket was wet. There was water from the rain on my face still.

Then her blue eyes were before me and I was looking directly into them. I wondered for a moment where she had been that night. Hiding, probably. She looked cautiously up at me, studying my eyes, frowning and irritated.

"I was just going to say that if I found a piece of paper and pencil in the dirt I was going to write you."

The expression on her face was the same, but she was studying me.

"But okay," I said with a shrug, with a scratchy resonance to my voice now I hadn't planned, with complete calm. "I won't write you. Even if I do find a piece of paper and a pencil in the dirt."

She looked back at me now.

"Have a good summer," I said.

Something came to her eyes, and she turned her glance downward, acknowledging the box without looking directly at it. She looked up at me, her head frozen in position.

"See ya'," I said just above a whisper, my voice gravelly.

I walked away down the hall.

"Hide them," she called after me. The sound of it reminded me of the cry of an upset cat.

I stuck the box further under my arm up into it against my ribs. I walked out, down the steps out into the rain and stood for a moment on the paved sidewalk, a bare outdoor light shining above behind me. I looked down now at the box of white roses, fingering the damp cardboard.

A dumpster stood nearby, but rather then chucking them I decided to take the flowers over for Jenny Havermeyer. The house where she lived was not far away.

I entered the silent house and walked quietly up the stairs to the third floor. I got up to the landing on the top floor, but couldn't tell which of four rooms was hers. I went back outside and opened the cool white box and spread the white roses over the wet grass in a place underneath what I guessed to be her window.

I walked back through the rain.

I took the bus out the Boston the next day, taking the T over the river at dusk into Cambridge, walking from Harvard to Inman Square past the two Italian sub shops, past the bathtub Madonna, to the house on Prospect Street where my brother lived with his old college buddies. We went out that night to the club my brother liked. I drank beers, watched the people dancing under the dim flashing lights.

My brother came up to me. "Did you tip the bartender?" I found him bearing over me. "She says you didn't tip her," he said quietly.

"I was going to. I thought you did that at the end of the night." Otherwise it was sort of fake, I thought.

"No, you tip as you go along."

"Oh. Really I was going to. You told me about tipping."

"Yeah, bartenders have to make a living too. And it's not cheap living in Boston."

I tipped the same young woman behind the bar who had brought the beers to me—I had three up to that point—five dollars for the Rolling Rock beer she gave me. "I'm sorry…" I began to say, but she nodded and turned away. She was busy, but later she wouldn't look at me in the same way she had avoided it. I slipped into a corner and watched the people dance again.

I watched a tall handsome man with tight curly excellently cut hair spin a tall woman with beautiful broad hips on the dance floor. He smiled broadly, his teeth shiningly white against the darkness of his brow, and she laughed and tilted her head back, the ruffles of her top held by elastic above her breast line, the tops of her hip bones there under her smooth tanned belly.

I took a look around the four walls of the dance floor and past the gray rhinoceros statue with shiny metallic flakes that stood close to the far wall. Three girls passed along the wall, drinks in hand, following quickly one after the other, laser lights shining off the ball spinning after them. I looked up again and they were in the corner already laughing with two thin guys in low-slung jeans. One girl, a tall brunette, stood with her pelvis forward, her neck stretching forward, her shoulders slouched as she talked with her friends about something, oblivious of me as I walked by.

I drank another beer. Another beer and maybe I would feel like saying something funny to someone I had never met before. Another drink and I would be my humorous old self again.

I walked home with my brother. We stopped for a slice of pepperoni pizza along the avenue, which I was grateful for. I was glad to be going home the next day.

The next day I got the bus back to Amherst. I gathered up my things in the dorm and my father came with the little white station wagon and picked me up. We drove back along the Thruway.

It had never occurred to me what a complete handicap it was to have humility. I suppose I had it in an honest way, some trick of chemistry, the effect of intellect, or from taking in my father's Buddhist thoughts. But it felt like a trap, like a wall set-up between me and other people.

You had to explain your vision to people. You might have thought they would simply understand, but it was as if they spoke another language secretly, or that you had to state it all outright and completely or they wouldn't understand, either because they wanted you to explain the whole thing as if it were some sort of exercise they thought would be good for you to complete, playing dumb as it were, or because they really weren't given to understand what you thought was perfectly simple and utterly logical and a matter of common sense.

Perhaps it is that you of all people were somehow the last person they would expect it coming from. Perhaps they hear the song of it from you and thereby take you as some sort of idiot; they look madly and completely elsewhere to find the wisdom you introduce; they look for it in news and on television and with all sorts of other friends who are simply not the kind to have such things within them; but all along it was you who had it, holding it gently as a child holds a flower, knowing instinctively it is something very true and beautiful. Maybe it is that they could never expect the richness of variation in your expressions of the truth, as if they truly thought that it would only be stated one way and that they could hear it one time and then after that beautiful moment of truth get very quickly bored with it and all the foolish impracticalities tied up to it.

I had so deeply liked how she had said that there should be an 'Aw, shucks' sign around my neck. But a part of that suggested that she took me as some sort of caricature of the Common Man, a Norman Rockwell figure come to life out of some idyllic small town painting not to be believed in any longer.

Well, they all thought Lincoln was an idiot too, never expecting Gettysburg, or the Second Inaugural. Then some crazy zealot put a bullet in his brain. Lincoln at least out grew his own innocence and fine illusions about people. It probably hadn't been so easy. Or maybe it was, just a lot of overkill, so to speak.

It wasn't a good sign if you couldn't explain yourself, or if it was that there was no one around to listen except a lonely dog with a friendly tail in the middle of the night. That made you wonder if your own stubborn pride hadn't gotten in the way. But didn't everyone know everything was just part of the spooky dream behind reality and that everything was for good reason in accordance with the universe? It was perfectly appropriate that she and I had ended up in the same class in some perfect little town not near anything going to college, a young man and a young woman poised for life. It made no sense fighting the Universe, and I hoped she would come to understand that.

But people are pigheaded and self-defensive after all, and they do have their own agendas, perhaps rightly so. What can you do? They have eyes, but cannot see.

The Princess would have the summer to think about things and learn the things I knew, assuming they were things she could understand and had a language for, and even cared to hear, as you can lead a horse to water, but fail in making him drink it. There was something about her, a forlorn quality, a familiarity with being alone, that I respected.

Maybe, like Jesus, you could feel when your benevolence passed out of you, as when someone touched his robe. Maybe the good would pass out of you and that by being brought into the world suffering would come your way. But that suffering would not matter as there was benevolence within you inherently and it would come out by and by, as a natural course of events in the world.

I had brought flowers to a girl and mumbled about drawing in the dust as if I remembered Jesus at the stoning. Perhaps it would sink in and become itself a part of the sad beautiful dream.

CHAPTER FOUR

It was cool in the early morning, under a clear sky. We came out of the big high-roofed corrugated shed to the lot, dump trucks, vans, pickups, big gang mowers, back hoes. Jack Peterson stood gassing up his mower, a lit cigarette perched in the corner of his mouth.

"Hey, Jack, can't you read?" Messina called, his thick bare arms folded across his chest, his legs straight beneath him.

Big Jack took a hit off his cigarette and flicked it from the end of his fingers over at Messina. The butt landed harmlessly and rolled on its side faster and faster down the sloping tarmac making its escape. We laughed and Tom and I climbed up into the open bed of the light blue long-bed truck. Kenny started her up. We followed the other trucks out of the yard, rolling downhill, turning right, past the golf course before us, then the new Astroturf soccer field below the road.

The truck pulled into the yard. We climbed down and went around side to the back door of the stone cabin. I got out the hose and watered the burlapped root balls of the saplings and shrubs, the spray making rainbows, the smell of wet gravel rising. We tossed the heavy iron rakes and shovels into the small trailer of the Cub Cadet tractor. We were shoring up the shale paths in parts where the spring runoff had washed them out. It was dark in the woods, silent, the underbrush holding the damp.

The trees shaded the slopes of the Glen. Fresh air came up from the stream. Leaves stirred in the treetops. The thick grooved bark of the tall wet tree trunks ran up through the shadows of the forest. A blue jay shrieked. I walked along behind the trailer, my leather boots pink from the shale dust. We arrived at the dump, where the shale pile was, hidden in shade and tall weeds. We each took a shovel and started away on the pile.

At lunchtime we brought the tractor back up the hill to the barn. Kenny pulled up in the new blue Chevy pick up with Hamilton College painted on the side in yellow letters. He brushed his mustache with the side of his finger in anticipation of something. He liked my term for smoking marijuana. "Botanizing," he'd say with a broad grin. He was a good guy. A friend of mine.

We got back to the lot with the big shed. I walked into the coolness of the garage to the crew room. My lunch was in the refrigerator next to the soda machine.

I sat on the hood of an abandoned blue Pontiac Bonneville, leaning back against the windshield. I opened up the brown paper bag, inspecting it. Dad had made us sandwiches. Today it was a roast beef with horseradish. I took a sip of ginger ale from the can.

There was a bleach-blond woman on the cleaning crew, attractive, tall with nice wide hips. Her crew came in a little while after we did. I was waiting for her. I kind of felt her look over at me as she walked up to the shed. There was something girlish about her when she did, and I thought that was very sweet.

Early in the summer we came in for a break in the dining common and she was having coffee with her crew. Kenny made a big deal about noticing her. Her husband, a big guy with a beard, had joined them. He came to pick her up in a Mercury Cougar at the end of the day, standing, not talking to anyone, watching her when she stepped out of the van. He came up along side her and walked with her the whole way to the shed. I could feel she wasn't happy. He was the reason why she was quiet, and it didn't seem like a good quiet. You can feel a lot about someone. You're not sure what to do with it, but you feel it. I thought she needed help. I wanted to help her. The guy made me nervous, the way he looked around from under his brow while looking straight ahead.

I wiped the crumbs from the hairs on my chest and ate my apple. I leaned back with my eyes closed.

I got up, stretched and walked back to the crew room. There had been a walking-stick bug on the Kousa dogwood bushes we had taken out by one of the Kirkland-side dorms the day before. We put the cuttings on the back of the truck, and when we drove up to the shed, the bug had come out and climbed onto my cap, fresh and green. The insect moved slowly, circumspectly, part plant, part animal. We left it with the branches on the truck, and now I wished that I'd taken it and let it go somewhere safe, as the pile ended up in the dump.

I walked back in the garage and I saw Messina talking to Wanda from the painting crew in the hallway. "Hey," he said to me. "Why don't you go rob a bank? What are they going to say? 'Oh, some handsome guy came in and took our money.'" He shrugged, imitating the daintiness of a female bank clerk. "But if I did, they'd have me behind bars in ten minutes. 'Big ugly guy with a scar on his face…'." I laughed and we went in to the crew room.

68

The crew came back in one by one to the crew room, taking their chairs. We were sitting still, legs out straight, hats tipped forward. Crane, a tan-colored man with a white tee shirt and chinos, came back in, peered around and gave his progress report and told us where we were going again. Then we filed out again silently and Kenny drove us back down to the barn at the Glen entrance.

We sat down in the meadow after spreading out the last shale load. There wasn't any point at Two Forty-five to go get another. I leaned back, not minding the light dampness in the grass, looking at the tulip poplar tall above. A hummingbird came and made his rounds carefully through the honeysuckle like he was playing a musical instrument.

At three fifteen we had the iron tools cleaned and back in the stone barn. After the freshness of the meadow the dry bone-meal fertilizer smell hung thickly about like forgotten death. We went back to the shed and punched out. My father came, and we drove back down College Hill. College Hill Road straightened out before you and you could see College Street, leading to the bridge over the Oriskany Creek, beyond the blinking traffic light at the foot of the hill. The brick cupola and spire of the town library rose above the woods. The houses passed by, and there wasn't anyone outside in the yards.

We went grocery shopping down at *The Jolly Butcher*. I looked over the meats behind the glass at the butcher's counter, red and cut neatly, the loins wrapped with string, a roll of butcher paper by the scale.

We got back to the apartment and Dad went out to walk Cricket. I watched them from the window as they walked into the field. The apartments were in the flats, with nothing but cornfields behind them. I would have felt like going for a walk, but there was nothing that was interesting. The creek was just up the road, with a highway bridge over it. The banks were steep and choked with burdocks. There was a small run-down bungalow in need of paint off the road. Behind it there was a *Karmann Ghia* that never moved. I wanted to check it out but the quiet of the house and the overgrown dirt driveway kept me away.

I stripped off my work clothes and took a shower, shaving in front of the mirror.

I heard them come up, the short-legged dog galloping up the stairs, refreshed by her walk. Dad opened the door and the dog shook herself and snorted when she came in, then snorted again at the carpet, smiling afterward, her tongue loosened, making a 'kuh, kh, kh' sound, a hint of slobber in her jowls. She took a drink of water from the bowl by the fireplace. Dad put the leash aside on the mantle and went into the kitchen to cook dinner. He had me cook when it was spaghetti with tomato sauce and sausage, and the garlic bread wrapped in tin foil in the oven, but tonight was not spaghetti night. I came through the living room where the television was on to MacNeil-Lehrer.

"Smells good, Dad."

"Chicken a l'Orange." It was Tuesday, time for a treat.

"Great."

"Get yourself a beer in the fridge."

"Okay."

I stood looking out at the cramped little deck outside the sliding glass door.

It all felt really strange to me. I had hoped for some miracle that would let us stay and keep the old house. I had difficulty accepting the summer before that it was coming to an end. Here, the apartments, painted the drab brown and green of vinyl-sided pre-made tool sheds, reminded me of Soviet housing I'd seen in *The National Geographic.* Up on the second floor here, with only a balcony, and Mrs. Abriel's Hallmark Card door below us, we were sealed off. The shag carpet didn't make up for anything. Things outside seemed like stiff plastic, untouchable, like someone else's backyard. Some of the yard was the butcher's backyard. The grass grew sparsely on the hard-packed ground.

We sat down at the dinner table, the chicken in the traditional yellow casserole dish.

"Dad, tell me about the Treason of the Clerics."

"Well, during the war, for example, science departments did their part in the war effort. In developing radar, new plastics, even in building the bomb... After the war they served the economy. In the post-World War Two era, academic institutions began to rely on corporate funding. Universities involved themselves more and more in research that served business needs." He paused and sat back in the wooden chair that went with the dining room table. "And this influenced the kind of scientist a university wanted to hire and keep around. If money and recognition came in for the research thoroughbreds, rather than a good science instructor, let's say, then universities would grant tenure accordingly. And even the entire structure of science departments changed. That's what happened to the Botany Department at UMass. It's all Microbiology and Genetics now."

"Okay. So that's the treason?"

"The purpose of the clerics, in our case, educators, is to aid young people in their quest for spiritual development. The fundamental intention of a liberal arts education is for the student to find his own talents, to find out what his dreams are in the course of making him well-rounded. But if all the instructor cares about is research and publishing, it's not the same sort of thing."

"So if I find out what my dream is…"

"You're good at what you like to do."

"But I always hear people say, 'well, it's a job.'"

"You're not going to be good at something you don't like to do. You may be competent at it, you might even perform well at it, but it's not going to make you happy."

"Does liberal arts still exist?"

"Yes, it does. But a college can become a place for vocational training, doing not much more really than preparing a student for a career in a particular line of work. It might be brain surgery, for instance."

"But people want to succeed. They want to make money."

"Yes," my father said. "That's how they think about it. That's the way the economy has made it."

I thought about it for a while. "That could really screw things up."

My father nodded. "Yes, it could."

"It could totally take humanity off whatever positive track it might be on, and just become this cold world where everyone works for the economy and there's no higher meaning or beauty or anything like that. I mean, like every decision a person makes, to love, to have children, it would all become for economic reasons."

We had our little cups of coffee and I thought about it some more.

"It just seems like there's no use for it when you get out into the real world. Like maybe I'd want to be a writer, but when I get out there... how?"

My father kept a noble silence on the matter for a little while. And then he said, rather quietly, "you'll find your way."

After we had coffee, I went into the kitchen to clean the pots and pans in a sink of soapy water. Dad put the dishes into the machine and then the machine began to make its peculiar wet groans, building up steam. He sat in the brown chair with the New York Times, the floor lamp beside him, the dog at his feet. I lay on my bed, head propped up, reading *Big Sur*.

"Is Billy Frank around?" my father said above his newspaper. This was his way of telling me it was okay to go out.

"I don't know, Dad."

It was a mild evening, the green of the lawns golden, then hushed into shadow, then the sky all lit above. I walked out to the Rok. I could hear the humid thump of the drums of the marching band practice from the high school parking lot. The humidity was sort of like salt and pepper, the way it colored the dusky light on the light brick of the high school.

I went into the barroom through the open door and ordered a beer. I watched the baseball game on the television at the end of the bar. The regulars wanted to hear the Yankees game so the jukebox, by the front door, was off.

I walked home later, coming in quietly to the apartment, across the shag carpet to the kitchen. The dog, resting on her side, raised her head up and looked at me out of the corner of her sleepy eye. I bent down to her and she lifted her leg up to be rubbed on the stomach.

"Hello, Cricket," I whispered. "It's not like Ernst Road when you could be outside at the end of the driveway all day, is it."

The dog looked away.

"Yeah, I know it. I feel the same way, too." I sat down next to the dog. "Maybe I won't go to work tomorrow."

I went to my room, walking past the open door of my father's bedroom, hearing him breath heavily, stopping for a moment to look in on him. He slept on his back usually. I laid there in the dark. The rooms were close together in the apartment. It felt to me like a camping trip that had gone on a long time, not that that was necessarily bad. It just was.

I thought about the girl. I wanted to write her letters. I wanted to, very much, but I didn't know what to say yet. There was something about her that told me she liked me seriously. I had a sense of her needing me, me in particular, to help her, like to save her from something. I sensed that she had to be harsh with me as she had been because she needed a lot from me. She needed me to be good. That she was that way—you could describe it as coldness, if you didn't know—meant she liked me very seriously.

I felt this attraction to her beyond myself. It wasn't my idea, nor my own will really. It was if we were pieces very much alike, with minor outside differences, falling into place by relationship with one another. A part of it was that she couldn't give me anything that would let me show it to anyone else. She couldn't give me anything by which I could go to someone else as proof that she liked me. So if anyone thought I was crazy for pursuing her, and going completely overboard, I couldn't disprove him. I could say it was a feeling I had, but who would believe that if they didn't want to? I could see it all before my eyes plain as day and understood it all perfectly. I realized that if I had any doubts about whether she liked me, it was from the skepticism inherent in people trying to make their way forward in the world in an unenlightened fashion, all that bleeding over on me, bringing doubts to my mind.

Even as I lay alone there, I felt this bond between us, as if we'd been created as something like brother and sister, kept apart for a long time, brought back together. It was a feeling in my chest, in the backs of my eyeballs, and everywhere else. And it was like I had to keep with the secretive nature of it, and suffer my loneliness quietly without wanting any other girl. I had to keep it quiet, but I had a sense, a vision sort of, of reward for keeping my feelings for her and for keeping the affair between us silently. One day she would give me all sort of treats and presents, like fish out of a bucket for a trained seal who had balanced a beach ball on his nose for so long. I liked it that it was a secret, I truly did, and I couldn't tell if she wanted me to write her or not. I guessed that I was supposed to pretend I was hurt, not about to write her any letters, that such would keep the perfect understanding a secret only we'd know. If I thought about it carefully enough, things were really coming along perfectly.

But I wanted to write her and tell her about the rain pouring over the eaves on the shed. I wanted to tell her about a lot of things.

In the morning I woke at the usual hour, feeling groggy, had toast and coffee with my father, neither one of us saying much, squinting curiously out the sliding glass door to speculate on the weather. We drove up to work. College Street was very quiet in the summer, then the hill rose and we went up it and around the bend.

We worked in the Glen that day. I mowed the Hemlock Enclosure in the afternoon when the sun was on it, a sloping long diamond of lawn ringed by a seven-foot tall hemlock hedge with plantings off the cut edges.

That night I drove down to the Rok, parking behind it not far away from the grand old ginko tree with all its reaching arms, the only survivor from a public garden that was now a supermarket parking lot. I felt the emptiness of the bar room, as if it were a stage-set, hollow props, fake facades, everything trying to advertise something at you. There wasn't anyone I wanted to talk to. Bob O'Donnell was away teaching at soccer camp. The only girls there were the pretty ones with alluring eyes on the calendars and the beer advertisements, the *Mikita Tool* gal in the men's room lit by a single bare light bulb. I watched the bartender work, then stop and smoke a cigarette. Someone called him on the pay telephone. I ordered another beer from him and then it was time to go home. I didn't even want to be there anymore. I wanted to be writing a letter to the Princess.

The town felt the same way as I drove past the sleeping houses. I put the accelerator down a bit heavier than usual coming off Elm past the cider mill onto Kirkland coming to the curve.

I got to the curve. I turned the wheel perfectly, as I always did. The car began to drift rather suddenly, sickeningly and quickly across the road. I turned the wheel into the skid. The car slid off the road.

I turned the wheel quickly back straight, pumping the brakes. The car flew past a telephone pole, cutting through a thick metal guy-wire brace. I had the car going straight now, sailing over the grass, not seeming to touch the ground. The car felt tiny, hurtling through actual space as if a sudden terribly strong wind had caught it in its soundless grasp.

The car sank back down as it careened forward. I pumped the brakes again hard, and finally the wheels caught. The nose of the car was down, sliding forward still.

The car came to a stop in the front yard of a small square house, just past an ornamental fruit tree.

I found myself sitting in the car, a loud clacking noise from the under the hood. I turned the key off. I undid my seat belt and opened the door. I stood looking at the bare metal showing through the paint along the big crease across the hood. The left headlight and the radiator grill were crushed inward, like teeth that had been pushed in.

"Fuck," I said.

I got back in and tried to start the car. A rapid clapping noise came from within the engine and I turned it off, putting my head down on the steering wheel. A light was on within the house. I couldn't tell if I'd had been on before. I heard a dog barking sleepily somewhere far-off in the night.

I walked the short distance toward the apartment. I crossed the road and came over the lawn toward the front doors no one ever used as the parking lot was behind. My father was sleeping. I stood outside the room for a moment, and then I came in and tapped him on his shoulder. His eyes opened. He came awake.

"Dad, I messed up the car. I... lost control coming around a curve and now it's... the front end has a big dent in it."

My father lifted himself up quickly, suddenly up, his eyes wide open. "Where is it?"

"Just up Kirkland. Five houses up."

"Can we move it?"

"I don't know. I don't think so."

In a matter of moments he had pants on and a shirt and his slip-on Wellington boots. He put on a woolen outer shirt.

"Let's see if we can get it back."

He took a quick stride through the wet grass. I followed him.

"I'm sorry, Dad."

"No, accidents happen."

We came upon the car. There was a moment of doubt on his face. "Let's see if we can get it back to the parking lot."

The car started up clattering. Dad shifted it into drive without hesitation and with a dragging noise we crossed the street without stopping, safely in the drive of the apartments and into the parking lot.

"Should we call the Police?" I asked.

"We'll worry about that in the morning."

"Dad, I'm sorry. I was going too fast."

"No, that's all right. That's what insurance is for. Things will go on just the same tomorrow. Get some sleep, and we'll take it step by step," he said quietly, sitting in his chair, taking off his boots. The dog came up and sleepily licked his hand.

"Okay, thanks Dad."

"Good night."

"Night."

I lay on the bed with my clothes off for a long time before falling asleep, the accident replaying itself, different parts, for a long time. It felt like something that wanted to make you cry, but that you could only cry actually now in the fresh recentness, that the crying would be submerged deeper and deeper as time passed, but that you would always feel it in such a way, just that the great shock of it made you entirely removed from it just as when it had happened. I got up and got a glass of water, peeking in to see my father quiet, breathing deeply. I couldn't tell if he was sleeping.

My father called the Sheriff's Department in the morning and we met the town cop at the scene. He was an affable beefy man with a trimmed mustache, shaking hands with both of us, going back to the car to talk into the radio. He came back with a clipboard and asked me to walk him through what happened. I took the cop up the street to where the skid had started. There was gravel spilled on the road.

"Well, I was coming back after having a beer at the Rok, and I was going a little bit too fast around the curve and the car spun out and I came down this side of the road on the grass." My mouth felt dry.

We looked at the tire marks where the car had stopped. We walked back toward the car. I had no idea what was going to happen.

"Well," the cop said, looking me over, "I think he's learned his lesson."

I nodded.

"You're not going to be going too fast next time around that curve, are you, young man."

"No, sir."

"Thank you, Officer Downey," my father said.

"Take care, gentleman."

The cop pulled up his belt and sauntered with a bit of lightness back to the patrol car, sitting there for a moment with his clipboard, the door still open, his leg out before shutting the door and driving off. I stood in front of the small house, looking at the tire marks. I didn't know if I should bring in some soil and plant some grass seed.

My father called a tow truck, which came later and hoisted the car up onto its flatbed, pulling it up with a chain. They were taking it to the auto place behind the Arena.

The mechanic, a gaunt blond-haired kid with an oily jacket, drove us out to a car rental place just off the Arterial heading into Utica. I didn't feel like talking much. "It might be totaled," the mechanic said. "I don't know how much the frame is bent."

"Oh, great," I thought. I looked out over the lot. Dad picked out a gold four-door *Volare*. There wasn't much to choose from.

"A real clunker," he said when we got on the road back to Clinton. "The Gold Bug." I had a little laugh, and felt like we were in a Mark Twain adventure, me and him, which helped.

"You should call your mother when you get back."

"Okay."

"I know she'll be an alarmist. You'll just have to bear with her."

"Yeah."

We came back to the apartment. I sat down in the brown chair next to the phone, feeling ill.

"Hi, Mom."

"Oh, hi, Jamie. Shouldn't you be at work?"

"Taking the day off today."

"Why?"

"Well, I got into an accident with Dad's car driving home last night. I'm fine, no one else was involved, no damage, just the car."

"Wait a minute. You... you were in an accident."

"Yes. I was coming around a curve going a bit too fast..."

"Oh, my God. Where were you coming from?"

"The Rok. But I didn't have that many, really."

There was silence. "Darling, if I ever lost you, I don't know what I would do," my mother said, coming back to the phone.

"I know, Mom."

"So you had too much to drink and you were speeding."

"No, it's not quite like that.   I... if I had more to drink I would have been more careful."

"Jamie, that's awful. If you had more to drink you wouldn't have been going that fast?"

"No."

"Sweetie, do you know what drinking does to you?" She was talking louder now, building momentum.

"Yes."

"Alcohol interferes with your judgment. That's in its very nature. So don't tell me... how could you say that... that if you'd had more to drink, you'd..."

"I know. It sounds screwy."

"Oh, do you think so? Do you know we could have lost you?! Do you know that when a car goes out of control it can hit things?"

"Yes."

"What happened to the car?"

"Well, it's in the shop. It hit a guy wire, so the front end... that's where the damage is."

"A guy wire? To what."

"To a utility pole."

"And how close did you come to the pole?"

"Not close."

There was a pause.

"Jamie, how do you think I feel?"

"Not so good. Scared."

"Yes, dear. I almost lost my son."

"No, you didn't. There's not a scratch on me, I was wearing my seat belt, I got the car back straight."

"You were lucky. We all were lucky, all of us, that we didn't lose you."

"Yeah, I know."

"No, if you knew you wouldn't have been driving your father's car like a daredevil. If I lost you I wouldn't know what to do with myself."

"I guess having a few beers didn't help."

"No, honey, it didn't."

After I put the phone down we ate lunch. The liverwurst was fresh and pink between the thick white bread, horseradish underneath the lettuce.

We were driving into town. The sun was coming through the windshield. Mom had been yelling at Dad yesterday afternoon. I didn't know what it all meant. But I didn't think it was right for Mom to get like that.

I was looking out the window when she began. "I'm not crazy, am I? I'm not going crazy. I didn't overreact with your father, did I?"

She looked over at me, her eyes asking me to tell her she wasn't crazy and that it was right for her to be so angry with Dad.

"No, Mom. You're not going crazy," I said, and then I looked out at the street before us.

"Am I a bad person?" she asked.

"No, you're not a bad person."

"Let's drive out to Unadilla Forks," my dad said.

"Okay," I said.

We went down to the car and my father said, "why don't you drive."

A pleasant sunny day spread itself across the mid-morning sky. It felt like a Sunday, and I knew we would pass along the big hills. They were nowhere near to being mountains, but down along the way out there they rose up bigger and stronger than the ridges of our town. We drove up Paris Hill, and then across several valleys, and then we finally were going up the hill where a colleague of my father's, an Englishman, lived in a barn. One end of it. He had kept animals, a goat, a couple of fat rabbits in cages, a calf, an excitable dog with pink-rimmed eyes and very tightly wound with muscles, but everyone was gone now without a trace. I remembered how the Englishman's girlfriend had put me up on a pony and walked forward with me in the field across the road. We'd looked for mushrooms in the woods back when Nancy Jaffe was alive.

Then we came back, and by the time we were coming back into our own valley, the college chapel's white steeple rising near the top of the ridge, I felt okay about driving again. My dad said nothing about it.

The next day I went back to work. The men had noticed that we were in a different car.

In the crew room waiting for the bosses to come in Messina nodded.

"Hey, what's up with the new car?" he asked, his muscular arms folded across his barrel chest, his hat tipped low over his head to lend a certain privacy to our conversation. The new car was funny enough by itself.

"Aah, I got into a bit of an accident coming home from the Rok." It was appropriate to confess.

"Uh oh," Messina said, smiling understandingly under his hat.

"Yeah, I was going around that curve on Kirkland by the town shed and slid across the road. I got past the telephone pole but it went right into the guy wire. Pow. I snapped it. I tried to keep it straight."

I looked up at the slight smile on his face. The scar across his cheek was reassuring, benevolent wisdom concentrated in a brotherly way.

"But I guess it was just luck that I didn't hit anything else."

There was silence in the room, the men listening.

"I tried steering it, but maybe I overcorrected."

"How bad's the car," asked Pinhead.

"Well, it's pretty banged up in the front end. The mechanic said the frame's bent. It's a unibody, so that will take awhile to fix, if it's not totaled. It was a lemon anyway. One of those Canadian-made Fords that was a piece of crap as soon as Dad drove it off the lot."

I shrugged at the laughter in the room from the men at different corners.

"My mother had quite a shit-fit about it."

"The old man?"

"Oh, he's cool. We talked to the town cop the next day. 'Well, guess he learned his lesson.' Left it at that."

The supervisor Roy Crane came in and I bowed my head down fixing the brim of my hat. There was an unusual quiet.

I was just about to get into the Chevy Pickup #32 when Burt Fuller came by walking toward the big light blue gang mower with its mowing wings up.

"Hey Crash, take it easy, all right," Burt Fuller said, turning back straight-ahead.

"Shit, I'll try." I smiled and looked over at the Harley he rode parked across on the other side of the paved lot, its windshield sparkling in the sun. It looked like a motorcycle cop's bike.

"Hey-ey, Kenny," he called. He liked to call out Kenny's name. I watched him as he climbed onto the big mower, blue work wear and tan leather boots. "Weepin' Willa," the man said in a musical voice, seeing Pinhead rolling along by on the little blue mower, his boots up on the running boards. Pinhead turned his head, crossing his eyes, a big goofy bug-eyed look spread across his face. Pinhead had straight blond hair that came out from under his cap when he hadn't just gotten a buzz cut. But it wasn't just the hair that evoked a willow tree, I thought.

Later that week I took the Gold Bug out up the old road where the house was. A Bruckner symphony was on the radio. I came up the first hill and parked by the fence that ran along the bank of the reservoir. I turned the car off and walked down to the break in the chain link fence near the dam. It was getting dark out now, the sky purpling and deep blue. Bats were out above the water flying in erratic direction, diving, turning abruptly over the great pool ringed by pines. I heard the water spilling down the breakwater. I walked out onto the dam, hearing a frog splash, disappearing as I came toward his post.

I stood on some earth and rocks of the bank, looking down into the water.

Jesus gazed down into the water. He saw the beauty of life, his childhood and all his acts, and each made sense by another. He gazed down and there were fish in the water and he saw them all and they were his brothers, looking up at him wonderingly and nervously with their fish eyes, turning away with a silver flick of the tail then coming back. And because it was his life and because he almost understood it perfectly he knew that one day soon he would put his foot out on the water and that it would hold there on the surface, that he could step out upon it.

And the fishermen looked from their fires, the sparks rising in the breeze from the lake, up from their nets at him standing there on the shore, contemplating, still, and they shrugged and winked, a smile between them, a nod of the chin in his direction, as if to say, 'what's he thinking about?' And Jesus felt it in his feet what the top of the water would be like, knowing all that it held in its depths. The fishermen went back to their mending and their humming, but it struck each of them, the poise of the man standing there.

The hair stood up on the back of my neck and I stood there carefully. A pair of dragonflies skimmed along, wheeling in opposite directions.

I drove past the house. The lights were on, but only a few of them. It looked unoccupied, as if an ill humor, poor digestion had taken over. I wished the girl were with me, so I could have told her all about the house and show it off, even if we didn't live there anymore. I wanted to go stand in the yard. I wanted to be underneath the trees.

It had been my job anyway before but now that it wasn't going so well between Mom and Dad I was very careful about mowing the lawn. I was careful around the dogwoods and under the yew bushes and sometimes I mowed the grass two ways, raking it in between. I wanted the yard as it came down from the four big old sugar maples along the road to be smooth and clean like a golf course right up to where you wanted it to remind wild.

At night after dinner I'd go out and check on the lawn. The swamp was behind me and I'd look in through the long windows and the light was warm inside on the books and on the high cedar ceiling that went up to the top of the split roof. My father would be reading on the brown chair, the dog by his feet. Mom would be quiet by then, watching the television after the news. It was warm and the grass was fresh and moist under my feet but not wet, all laid out before the night and the sounds from the swamp and the stream out back.

Sometimes I'd go and walk up the road in the night, the surface of the road warm and very quiet. I'd go up the dirt and pebble road to Chuck Root's field. I'd look back and see the glow of our house standing above the woods in the little vale. It was our house. It was like a ship.

My mom came to pick me up for the weekend. She had me show her where the accident had happened. We walked over from my father's.

"Why were you going so fast?"

"I wasn't going that fast."

"You were going fast enough so that you lost control of a car going around a curve. You could just as easily have hit that telephone pole."

I was going to say, no, I could not have, but I kept my mouth shut. I had to admit I was fortunate where the pole had been positioned, that there weren't any trees along the road, no cars parked along the road on that side. I knew the curve, but there were things I was not in control of that night. A car parked in the driveway of the house where I'd come to a stop in front of would not have been pretty.

We drove out along Route Five. It was the slow way, through farmland, the green rows of corn standing tall now. We passed a farmhouse with a combine harvester with a for sale sign in its window in the yard. The countryside reminded me of the pictures I'd seen of where James Dean grew up in Indiana.

We had baked chicken breasts and potatoes for dinner with a salad and white wine. It was nice to drink wine after dinner and go look through the bookshelves. My mom had most of the old book collection. I was looking through the children's books when she came in and sat next to me on the couch.

"How's your father?"

"He's pretty good. He sits in the brown chair and reads *The New York Times*. He's acting department chairman now that Donald Preston is sick."

"He has cancer?"

"Prostate. He'll live, but he has to get treatment. Chemo."

"How long will your father stay on?"

"They keep asking him back. I think he said he can stay as long as he wants. But that he's getting tired of it."

"Does your father still like teaching?"

"Oh, yeah. And he'll tell me about his students, and have them by to talk during lunch hour."

"Your father is a wonderful teacher."

"I think there's a class the whole hockey team is taking."

"Someday you should go sit in on a class."

"It wouldn't throw him off?"

"No."

After dinner I went for a walk. There was a bar just up the street, but it looked quiet and I did not feel very adventurous. I went back to my mom's apartment and lay in bed thinking about Jenny Havermeyer, the time sophomore year I went down to the basement of the dorm to take a crap in one of the quiet bathrooms, one on each end of the dorm. On our side of the dorm the bathroom was the woman's restroom, while the other end was the men's. I didn't feel like walking down to the other end, and the basement was deserted anyway, so I went into the woman's room. I was sitting on the can in the closed stall when I heard the door swing open. "Hold on," I said, "I'm takin' a shit." I heard a light happy laugh, the sound of a beautiful woman's laughter, which somehow I could easily distinguish.

I thought of how I could sense that she liked me, how she heard me strumming my guitar in the stairwell, playing the *English Beat* song, "*Save It*

For Later." She liked me for who I was, for my own style. My roommates
had overheard her through the wall talking with her roommates about sex one
Friday night, about how they liked being thrown to the ground and kissed
forcefully, how guys always grabbed and held on tight to their asses when
they came. I had missed that night, the boys sitting around in the room where
the stereo was, hearing them through the fire door. I had been at the library.

Jenny Havermeyer was a beautiful girl full of life, full of juice, and
would never be dried out, never take on the look of a bony old horse ridden
into leather. I thought of her smile, her high breasts, the flesh of her tennis
skirted legs, the inviting shape and tautness of the inside of her thighs, the
sight of her walking away, her honey lightly-curling hair that reminded me of
the Roaring Twenties, all equally, eloquently saying the same thing. One of
her roommates came by toward the end of the year and asked me for my copy
of *The Catcher in the Rye*, as if I were the authority.

Sunday night after Mom dropped me off in front of the apartment
building I drove the Gold Bug up past the reservoir, past the old house, up to
the high point on Champion Road overlooking the length of the valley as it
ran south to Deansboro and Oriskany Falls. Further up the road, which
dipped down then up again rising past the Champion farm, the cows would be
out in the darkened whispering fields. I turned off the car and got out and
stood looking out over the valley.

I liked the smell of the fields at night. I could hear the wind through
the woods on the hill below. I looked up at the starry sky, uncompromised

by any modern electric haze, no cluster of lights to mar their shine, the only lights being distant lights across the valley, as from ships out in a harbor, each a small point of light signifying a house, a farm, a family. I could see a great distance over the ridge on the other side of the valley.

And then for a while again, for a moment again thinking about the Princess, the things that had come to pass did not matter. And all was good, I told myself.

Or rather, come to realize, life was not about happiness and easy answers, but about the other things.

CHAPTER FIVE

We drove in the sunshine along the New York State Thruway, the sky bright blue, puffy white picture-book clouds rising above the low long ridges distant from the road. The wide river came in and out of sight below the road where it climbed, mill towns down in the river valley, cows above us outside barns in muddy pastures. Closer to the river again we passed a row of three Victorian houses connected by telephone lines.

We came down quickly in traffic toward the Hudson, the city of Albany opening behind us downstream as we crossed the bridge. Then we climbed up to the eastern flats, the Catskills rising like smoke in the distance, finding the tollbooth ahead. The land changed as we passed into Massachusetts, the road along the lowland, climbing upward through wooded mountains in long steady angles.

We pulled up behind the old Deke House with the light of early afternoon coming over the hemlocks. My room was at the end of a short hallway on the second floor leading to treated pine steps out the back of the house.

"Well, let's get you settled," my dad said as he opened a door, reaching to gather my coats from the back seat. I opened the tailgate. My dad carried my guitar up to my room.

My father sat down in the car.

"I'll miss you, Dad," I said.

"I'll miss you, too," he said quietly, turning as if looking in the rear view mirror. He turned forward. The car began to roll, crunching the gravel.

I watched the car drift slowly away down the hill, and then it disappeared around the bend of the hemlock hedge.

I climbed the wooden fire escape stairs to the hall. I looked out the window of my room. I went up the hall to find the bathroom. The open balcony above the main stairwell had been closed in with safety glass. I gave it a tentative kick with the heel of my sneaker.

I took a walk through town and up toward the quad. I saw her from a long distance as she bounded up the stairs of the little hall near Frost Library. She came out, white registration packet in her hand, slipping quickly back down the steps.

Needles had fallen along the edges of the grass. I came to the quadrangle. I sat on a bench in front of the library. I watched a sparrow hop about beneath a yew bush, looking around, tiny little cones lying here and there.

I went back to the house on the hill and to my room in the back. It seemed more and more like a cell. I rummaged through my small collection of albums, and took out the Deutsche Grammophon Beethoven record and put it on the turntable, turning on the guitar amplifier that I used for a speaker. I put the plug from the turntable into the amp, then picked up the needle and put it over the record. The record began to spin. I put it the needle down at the beginning, *The Overture to Coriollon. The Ninth* was next. Down the hallway at the back of the house no one cared how loud I played it, and I gave the music the healthy respect it deserved, even if it was in mono rather than stereo.

A small piece of paper from my course registration packet, a blank form by which to arrange a course schedule sat on my desk. You wrote in the courses carefully in their respective meeting times, Monday-Wednesday-Friday, Tuesday-Thursday, the hour-long classes, the ones that went longer. Mine was blank and I had intended at first to throw it away. But now I looked at it. At the top you wrote your name in, then next to it your class, in case you forget or if you lost it and didn't know what to do with yourself until some kind person found it and returned it to you.

"Fuck you, you assholes," I wrote in the first line. "Leave me alone," I wrote in the next blank. I made up what I would be doing in the different time slots. "Pissing." Yes, that sounded like a good way to start on Monday. Followed by an hour of "Shitting." Why not. How about "Rolling in Vomit and Broken Glass." That would be good later in the week, in the Tuesday-Thursday eleven thirty to one slot. "Jerking off," yes, that would find a place. Fridays would be devoted to "Rye Whiskey," followed off by "Vomit' then "Death."

I taped it to the outside of my door, and went back in, closing the door behind me. There were some blanks still, which I could fill in as I thought of them. I had a poster of Andrew Wyeth painting, *Distant Thunder*, a woman lying in the grass, a dog nearby, a couple of pine trees beyond at the top of the meadow, a basket of blueberries in the foreground. It went kind of with a vision I had. In the woods, or in a meadow, far from a town, you can be yourself. You can be gentle and calm. Wyeth painted the grass and the trees and the light upon them with such care. It was like being outside. I put it up on the wall above the little bed.

The next afternoon I went to the music building. I went upstairs and found a free practice room. I couldn't play much, but I liked the piano, the way all the notes were laid out there in front of you, all equal. I plunked a few keys with a finger, listening. I put my hands down full, resting them across, then the little bit of Chopin's Funeral March I'd figured out, theme and interlude.

"*And at the end of the performance of the great final symphony the conductor of the orchestra turned the dark maestro to face the audience of the concert, as Beethoven could not hear and knew not of their admiring applause,*" I murmured to myself, picking out a few notes of *Ode to Joy.* "*And the composer beheld them standing now, beaming with the irrepressible joy his music had brought to their hearts.*"

Browning, a soccer player from my freshman dorm, stood down in the lobby, looking at a bulletin board of departmental course offerings. We passed through the glass doors out into the light and the air was warm again after being inside the dark building.

I saw her as I raised my head and looked forward into the sun. She stood facing me, turned from the conversation she was having with a balding kid of exaggerated good posture, also a sophomore. Her eyes followed me as I looked into her face, holding me in her sight as I came forward. She stood where the two sidewalk paths met, directly before me. I felt the closeness of our bodies. I felt how I was taller than she was. She looked down, and then looked up at me again, blinking. I came forward. She watched me coming toward her, looking slightly to her side as I drew closer.

I came up to her, passing beside her. "Hey, Jerkpot," I said, my voice stiff, tightened, my eyes straightforward. I slowly lifted my notebook and hit her lightly on the side of arm below the shoulder. She stood there, waiting for something. And then she was behind me.

We were at the dining hall when Browning looked over at me.

"'Hey, Jerkpot,' where did you come up with that?"

"Oh, I don't know. *Rebel Without a Cause*, I guess." We went in through the line.

"I brought her flowers at the end of last year," I said. I put the top of the bun down on my chicken puck sandwich. I thought now of how she had looked up at me, all of her, standing there.

"He's deaf. Don't you get it? He's deaf! Look, will you. Deaf."

She was sitting in one of the deep plush chairs in the lobby of the old library, one leg folded over the other. I came forward and sat down in the chair next to hers. The chairs were at an angle.

"How was your summer?"

"Okay," she said. She sat in her chair protected by the arms, sunken into the cushions. A small notebook sat closed on her lap.

"Did you work?"

"I was a receptionist." She raised her sight and looked over the carpeted room, white columns rising to the ceiling two floors above us.

"Did you like it?"

"You sit in an office and greet people." She looked down at her folder.

"I bet you're good at it," I said.

"It's not much of a challenge," she said, rolling her eyes privately, not looking over at me.

"And your parents, how are they?"

"They're fine," she said, her voice rising.

She looked back down.

"My Dad had an accident on his bicycle, but he's okay," she added, her eyes looking left and right without looking up. She raised one arm up on the arm of the chair. I looked down at the stripes of her French sailor's shirt.

"Oh, I'm sorry. "

"I think he hit his head, though he said he didn't. He was acting strange for a little while, but with him it's hard to tell."

"It must be hard riding in a city, with all the traffic."

"This was when we were out in the country."

"In Pennsylvania."

"Yes. He went off the road somehow."

"Oh."

"Into a ditch," she said.

"I'm sorry. I used to bike a lot myself."

"He watches television. Basketball, football, baseball. That seems to amuse him."

"My brother likes to watch sports on TV."

I took a look at her, as she was looking down at the folder on her lap.

"I wrecked Dad's car going around a corner. For awhile we had this crappy *Volare*."

She didn't say anything, but let out a smirk.

"Did you pick your courses out yet?" I said.

"No, I'm still trying to figure that out."

"Let me know if you need any help."

"Okay," she said.

Her hair had grown in. The front doors opened and a boy and a girl, both juniors, came in, laughing over something. Her eyes turned toward them.

"Are you unpacked yet?"

"Almost."

"Yeah, I'm almost done. Just putting up my posters."

She looked back down at the cover of her notebook. There was a slip of folded paper jutting out slightly, and she opened the cover slightly to put the paper back straight.

I stood and walked away.

Mom was yelling at my father. "You're a failure." Dad never raised his voice. He just sat there in the kitchen and took it while my brother and I sat in the television room watching Gilligan's Island. My brother could tune it out, his head propped up on a pillow from a mattress on the floor.

I couldn't take it anymore so I went down the stairs the cellar and took the garden whip from against the bare plywood wall. I had been through a few of them, braking their blades off, making a path from the backyard down to the stream, cutting through the little weed trees beneath the old apple trees. Rooting them out one by one would be too hard. I went down into the woods and whacked away at a path I had made some progress with. The snap weeds came up easy. The little trees were wet and green and it took time to cut through. I could hear Mom raising her voice still, and I could smell the laundry from the dryer vent behind the kitchen. I went and sat down on the moist dirt by the stream, where there was a small waterfall.

That evening I went to the meeting at the Chapel for prospective thesis writers, in the office of the chairman of the English Department. I opened the door. Twicknam, the chair of the department, sat on the top of his desk holding the edge of it with both hands as he leaned forward. He watched me come in and his eyebrows flared up as he looked me up and down.

He tossed his head back and looked down before him. Five students sat at the front of the room, taking turns about what they had all done over the summer, looked up at him eagerly when he spoke. His chin extended out over them, tipped with a beard, the bare skin of his head sun-tanned like the rest of his face.

"Well," he said, breathing in and then exhaling, "here we are. Let's get started." He leaned back, supported by his arms.

"Ugh," I said to Whacko when we walked out of the door on the quadrangle side of the Chapel after the meeting was over. The humidity had vanished in the breeze, and a hollow moan passed through the branches high above us.

"Like we were a bunch of chimpanzees."

Whacko laughed, inhaling each time.

"The advisee will bring his work into the advisor... the advisor will read the work... then offer critique. The advisee will then write more and bring it back... and then both will breathe together in and out as if anything either of them has said has the slightest importance toward anything that goes on in the world. Jesus, Whacko. You almost want to kick him in the teeth."

"Jeez," said Whacko, laughing, slightly distant.

We walked across the quadrangle, a light warm wind picking through the leaves at our feet. "I want to write about Joyce," he said, peering ahead nervously through his horn-rimmed glasses. We walked on a little bit toward the library. I liked the smell of leaves that time of year. I said I was going to walk home. I went back and pulled out *In Our Time* and read about Horton's Bay.

I had a few beers and later I called her. Her roommate answered. There was the sound of a hand coming over the speaker end, like listening into a seashell, muffling out all but the edges of giggling in the distance. Then she came to the phone.

"Hello, this is Jessica," she said confidently, with a slight inflection to act surprised, wondering who was calling her.

"So what are you doing tonight?"

There was a pause, as if others were listening.

"Just catching up with my roommates," she said, returning from something that had momentarily distracted her.

"I bet there's a lot to catch up on."

"So what are you going to do with yourself when you leave?"

"I'm going to be a novelist," I said.

"Oh," she said, pleasantly cool.

"And what do you want to be when you grow up?"

"I don't know," she said. "Perhaps a sociologist. But they don't make any money."

"As long as you're happy," I said.

"I'm selfish though. Honestly, it's the way I am. Once I went trick-or-treating with this girl in our building, and I convinced her to give me all her candy. A few years later she punched me on the arm. 'That wasn't fair,' she said."

"We're all selfish."

"You've picked a lonely profession. I guess that makes sense."

"I guess," I said. "Who knows? I just want to be honest."

"Well, I must go now," she said, her voice turning breezy and higher, as if a lighter matter had been placed before her.

"Okay."

The next day I went to the first class of Deviancy, in the auditorium of the music building. I came down the aisle to a row not far from the front, and shimmied in to the middle of the row. I was sitting there quietly minding my own business when I saw her coming down the row, followed by some Scandinavian-looking kid. She came up the row toward me. She drew her skirt behind her and sat down, one empty chair away. She turned partly toward me, looking down in front of her as if to say, "oh, what a surprise." She settled herself in her seat and assumed a silence, as if listening for something, waiting.

"What a nice red sweater," I said, not looking over at her.

"Oh," she said. "What was that you said?"

"I said, what a nice red sweater."

"Oh," she said, looking down into her shoulder bag, containing a smile, something passing through her body.

"You look nice in it," I said, quietly, slouched low in my chair.

"Thank you."

She sat down low in her seat, just as I had. She kept from looking over me, but for a quick glance, in that way people who are understood to be sitting next to you don't look over at you. She blushed slightly. I looked over at her and she had pressed her lips together, looking about in front of her without looking up above the row of seats before us.

I turned toward her, looking at the way her hair fell, the length, the color of it, having imagined it all summer until no longer being certain of what it looked like. I looked forward again. I felt her perk up, flexing her lower back just slightly, her knees up against the back of the red plush chair in front of her.

At the end of class I let her go down the aisle ahead of me, off with the sophomore kid she had come with, leaving me behind. I walked out of the music building to the walkway that led to the dining hall.

After dinner, I walked up through the quadrangle to the Chapel. The doors were open and I walked in and sat down in one of the pews. The lights were off. My eyes adjusted to the dark so I could make out the bearded faces of the oil paintings hung along the walls.

I put my arm along the top of the pew, stretched out. I couldn't study any more. I don't know what had happened. I couldn't write papers. I didn't know if I was going to make it through the year. I liked going to class still. I went to the library still, but it felt better to do something else, like go for a walk on some street I didn't know about. But I had walked all the streets of the town, late at night, and there wasn't anything new. There was a dog now and then who followed you for a while, recognizing something about you.

I didn't know how to pray, but I leaned over and put my hands together. I prayed for my mom and my dad. I prayed for the house. I prayed for myself. But again my thoughts turned to her, and I prayed that the best thing, the very best thing that could happen to her would happen.

I left by the front door of the Chapel. I sat down on the grass slope high above the road, my forearms wrapped around my knees, looking down at the solitary cars rolling by. You heard the sound of the tires on the road surface above the motor.

It was summertime and I was in the car with my mom, sitting in the back seat on the raised cushion. We were riding into town. I looked up at the hillside, the bricks shining golden through the swaying leaves of the trees up above. The sun hit the white steeple in the middle of everything. "Mom, Is that where Dad teaches?"

"No," my mom said. "That's the college. Your father teaches at the university."

"What's the difference?"

My mom laughed. "Well, that's where you get to go if you're very smart and very lucky. People of privilege send their sons there."

And I looked up at the hill as the hillside swung past outside the open window of the Volvo station wagon, a funny yellow building up on top of a round, then lower a solemn wide building with big pillars across a dipping lawn. I looked at my mom as she drove, looking forward at the street from behind her sunglasses

"I had a date once with a fellow who went to Amherst College," my mom said. "But then he forgot about me, I guess."

We went to go pick up my dad. We parked in a parking lot and went down some stairs and then up a hallway, the walls tiled yellow. I looked up at my dad and he looked down at me and smiled and what fine light hair he had on his head. Then I was very tired.

The light was golden like morning again as we passed by the hill again. And I wondered, how, really, do people learn, and what do they learn, and I knew it was a very fine thing to learn, and that I myself knew how to learn, and that one day, I would step up to such a place and begin, in earnest, my own voyage. It was not yet the time, though, as I sat in the back of the car, and I put my hand on the door of the car, as if to hold it, as it would support me my whole life. One day I would learn, and then I would teach, without fear of teaching, just like my Dad, standing tall in his suit in the morning, as I peeked from the closet.

A week went by and I called her. Her roommate Laura answered the phone. Then she came to the phone.

"Hi."

She let out a long sigh.

"Hello," she said, as if with an effort.

"Hello."

"Look, why don't we meet for lunch tomorrow at the dining hall," she spoke quickly, having calculated something. "We need to talk. I don't think you understand. You see..."

"No, that's okay," I said, before she could go on. "I don't get up very early."

There was a pause on the other end of the line.

"I never say anything anyway," I said. My voice had become low and scratchy.

"I'm just not the right one for you," she stated with confidence.

"Yeah," I said, my voice cracking, turning hollow right in the middle of it. I didn't have control over that. "I'll find the right girl someday."

There was another pause on the end of the line.

"See ya," I said. It came out hoarsely, whispered.

"Bye," she said, gently. The line was still connected.

"Bye," I said, and hung up the phone. And again, I knew what I had known all along, with her and with respect to everything else, that it wasn't just me, or some silliness, but a very real way I felt about something, something that was very sweet to hold on to, even if it was just some silly dream.

I went out and drank beer to get drunk at the usual Friday night house party. I looked on from a wall in a hallway as people floated past, catching up from the summer. New faces, blurs of conversations passed me by. I returned the plastic cup to my lips. Later I went up and watched two blond freshman girls, dancing a *Grateful Dead* dance together. They were cute, in a stocky way, and I drank from my beer cup, looking away, but following their happiness. I went up and said hi to them but they were busy, smiling at me but not saying anything. People will drive you to drink, just being around them.

I made it home by myself.

I woke up in my bed with a very dry mouth. The sun was shining fully into the yard outside the window. I cracked the stiff window open. It was warm again. I pulled on jeans and cowboy boots and walked slowly down to the dining hall, squinting and grumpy, the light powering down, the grass translucent green.

The dining hall was quiet, about to close. A chubby kid came in behind me. He looked up at me with his bulldog jowls, his eyebrows raised. I saw her come in behind the kid, picking up a tray from the stack, turning and putting the tray on the aluminum rails, facing forward, her hand on the tray.

"How's it going," I muttered to the kid behind me. The kid looked up. I got a plate of scrambled eggs, some bacon.

I tried not to look at her. I came out and placed my tray down on the shelf before the salad bar. I went looking for grape juice, over in the dining hall, East, on the other side of the entryway. I came back. She had vanished. I sat down and ate alone. I had thought she would stay. I could barely move anyway.

I walked back home, showered, shaved and put on a white cotton button up shirt, and preppy plaid wide-bottom slacks. I wanted to get a birthday card for my dad. I felt better now. It was good to walk into town, away from the college.

I walked down the main street to a gift shop before the gas station. I was looking through the Gary Larson *Far Side* cards, at one with a *Lone Ranger* theme, when I saw her browsing at the front counter. She came close by me. I let a judicious amount of time pass before I said anything.

"Hey," I said quietly, so as to not disturb her, glancing briefly at her then looking down.

"Oh, Hi."

She looked down at the silver jewelry in the display case, smiling before something.

"How are you?" she asked.

"Oh, fine," I said, smoothed over. I looked down and scratched the back of my neck. "My posters keep falling off the wall with all this humidity. I guess I need to find something that sticks them on a little bit better," I said.

"Yes," she said, laughing lightly, not looking up at me but aside at something in the shop.

I went back to the card section. She came over toward me, browsing.

"My Dad's birthday's coming up," I said, picking out the card I looked at before and opening it up again.

"Oh," she said, and smiled.

I lingered a little longer, putting the card back, poking around in the corner to stay longer. I looked back over at her. She was looking down at frilly open blouses, the same private smile on her face. She held one out on its hanger, pulling it slightly away from the circular rack it was on, smiling at it.

I went up to the counter and paid for the card. I looked back around to see where she was, but I didn't see her. She had disappeared. I left.

I walked up through town up to the main intersection, the Common before me, the college beyond it, the town hall below to the left. I passed under the oak trees and sat down on the steps of the town hall. It was warm, the sun on my shoulders, and I sat back. I watched for her to come by. Twenty minutes, thirty, passed and she did not come by. I got up finally, and walked back up the hill.

It was one of those summer days we were back visiting and I went with my mom to the new store down by the gas station. It was a hippy kind of store, incense, candles, a whirling electric weaving implement that looked like a small helicopter. I stood behind my mom, as she moved about. Then we were outside and met my dad and we walked around behind the gas station and the little row of shops and there was a cemetery. We walked through the grass and there were a few trees on a hill and some hemlock bushes. We walked up the hill and then we were standing by a little fence, a small family plot. My mom and dad looked down upon it, and each read aloud what it said on it. "Called Back," it said across the low little stone. Funny finding something like it behind the row of shops.

I went to Deviancy on Tuesday. I sat by myself and did not see her. "Uhm, Uhmm…" the professor vocalized, his chin held up to project over the auditorium of the music building, the pipes of an organ rising behind him brightly lit. "A society has its way of controlling individual behavior. It creates deviants… umm… separating them from its ranks," he called over the crowd seated in their plush red theater chairs. I took a few notes.

Later on I went and talked to Prescott in his office. I needed an advisor for my thesis.

"No, I'm not a Hemingway man. You should probably go to Carlson, I would think," Prescott said, his voice dry, looking away.

I went by Carlson's office on Friday, during his office hours. He had been assigned to me as my advisor when Duchamp went on sabbatical the year before. I stood in the dim light of the hallway, outside his door, hearing him talking. Finally I knocked.

"Yes. Come in," I heard through the door.

I poked my head in.

"Let me call you back," he said. "Yes. Fine. Bye," he said, putting the receiver back on the black rotary phone, smiling to himself, then leaning back with his hands folded behind his head. I looked around the books in the office and sat down in the chair before his desk. He looked up at me. His face had changed.

"Well, I'm interested in doing a thesis on Hemingway, the boundary in his works between fiction and non-fiction."

Carlson moved his seat back slightly. He looked down at a small space like a strike zone before him. Wearing jeans and a cotton turtleneck, he looked as if Robert Redford had dressed him.

"Who's going to be your thesis advisor?"

"Well, maybe yous, I was thinkin'," I said quietly.

"Mees?" the man said, grinning plastically, his lower lip out, his eyebrow raised and cocked in cleverness. "Well…" His eyes shifted left and then right.

"I uh, found your American Lit class very interesting."

"I remember you had trouble writing papers." Carlson leaned back and reached a hand around to the back of his head, raising his political chin.

I didn't say anything. I felt tired. I looked along the row of the neatly kept bookshelf behind him. I had written a good paper about a Hemingway story, "The End of Something." Yes, it was two weeks late, but I put a lot into it, because I cared a lot about the subject, everything about it. He had sent me a note back then about 'rapidly developing academic trouble.' Didn't make one comment on the paper. I got it back, nothing on it. Then I got my grade through the mail.

I looked at him. "I got one in a bit late."

"Sure," he said calmly.

"Okay, thanks a lot."

"So we'll see some writing from you?" He brought his reading half-glasses up to his nose, took a quick glance at matters on his desk, then looked straight at me.

"Yes, you will."

"Okay," he said, leaning forward, pulling his chair back to the desk.

"Thank you, sir," I said.

I stood and opened the door. An African-American girl had been waiting outside. I nodded to her. I stepped aside and she moved quickly and happily into the room. "Hello, Jock," she said. "I haven't seen you in awhile!" He stood up from his desk to hug her. I walked up the hallway, hearing the door close behind me. I sat down on the bench outside of Duchamp's office. Strange when people move on from your life.

Duchamp. The old man had hand-picked me as one of his two advisees when I came to college. I got the impression it was for a little piece I'd written about sitting by the old reservoir at the bottom of the road, how it was my little Walden Pond full of strange flying creatures. He raised me, he made me, that first year, the first semester, and then, strangely as he'd come, he let me go. It was as if he were saying, that I had to learn things on my own, that one day I would write in the sweet intellectual way of a Chekhov, very graciously, and with a tender eye toward humanity, but that he could only give me some raw material of a basic tool of making a moment something full, seen with open eyes and heart, the rest I would have to do myself through living. It had been a silent agreement between us. He would never say, here, here is some useful shortcut. He had perfect faith I would slowly take my time at it, and come upon it when I was ready, through patience, the only thing you really need to be a great writer, and a certain enjoyment over craft and talking to myself every day in the form of writing in a notepad whatever came to mind. It was as if he were subtly telling me that all I wanted to do would one day be graceful and easy, and that the ability had come to pass by being there all along, nurtured, in a way. And now he was sort of smiling at my beginning to learn things that he managed to keep himself free from, for he too was allowed, through his own way of being a great writer, not the perfect creature of modern institutional academic habit. While the exercise I was about to commence upon, while entirely futile, would be a form of a beginning.

The next Friday my brother called and told me he was coming out from Boston. He was coming out by bus with Deb, who had come out to visit him in Boston. Deb was going to Mount Holyoke.

"What time does your bus get in?"

"Around ten thirty I think."

"You want me to come pick you up down in Springfield?" I offered.

"That'd be great."

"I think I can borrow someone's car."

The next day there was a pep gathering to mark the beginning of the sports season. I poured beer at the outdoor fundraiser for the baseball team. A cute freshman that reminded me of the Princess came up to the table in her running outfit, but I could not persuade her to have a beer. I had a few myself and kept going 'til dinner.

I went home and took a nap. I woke three hours later. My mouth was dry. I looked at the clock.

"Shit."

It was quarter of ten.

I got the car keys from Hereford over at Love House, and went to the dirt lot below the house for the station wagon. The bus was getting into Springfield at ten, or was it getting into Amherst? No, Springfield. I was going to be late.

I saw a bus coming up the long hill as I drove out of town to get on the highway to Springfield. I got to Springfield, forty minutes later. There was no bus. I drove back to Amherst. The road was dark, not a car on it. Suddenly, road construction signs and orange arrows stood in the middle of the road in front of me. I swerved the wheel, getting through them on luck. My mouth was dry after that.

It was late by the time I finally got to the party, which was spread between the two big and elegant fraternity houses situated on the corner looking over the Common and up at the College. It was Homecoming weekend.

I walked in through the front door of PsiU. I saw her standing in the foyer. She turned her back and her friends stood around her expectantly. I looked at her back, her hair falling on her shoulders. The group paused, waiting for something to happen. One of her roommates, with curly blond hair, stood close by her side.

I passed by her, out the door, on my mission. I headed over the ChiPsi. The band was playing well, the room swaying as the bass played the sliding part and the singer started singing the opening to *Take A Walk On The Wild Side.* I found my brother by the side of the dance floor with Deb.

"Hey Jamie, where you been?"

"When did you guys get here?"

"Around ten."

"Oh, I thought you said you were getting into Springfield at ten. I drove all the way down there."

"No, we were getting into Amherst at ten."

"I got confused."

It had gotten too late and I had been distracted. I had wanted to dance with her. I had known that as soon as I heard the band. It would have been perfect. And I had fucked it up.

That night I lay on my side in bed, staring at the wall. I lay there. I tried praying. After a long time I fell to sleep.

The next night after dinner--it was getting dark out earlier—I saw her leaving the dining hall. I walked with her down to her dorm.

"Do you like Deviancy?"

"It's okay. Do you?"

"Well, I think it's good. The gay alumni they had the other day, they seemed pretty normal, just like you and me, really."

"I think you would like going to gay bars. There are a lot down in The City," she pronounced, chin in the air, her book bag over her shoulder.

We were at her door now. I stopped. "Oh," I said, flatly.

"You should go to one sometime," she said. She stood by the door, tossing her head back to look away, bringing her heels together.

I looked up at her for a moment. "Yeah," I said.

She looked off to the side.

"Good night," I said turning and walking away up the hill without looking back.

Three days later it was Halloween. I put on my dungaree jacket, Levi's and my cowboy boots. It was as close as I could get to *Cool Hand Luke*, escaping from prison. I went into town to the liquor store near the town hall looking for a prop, something appropriate for an escapee. I saw a bottle on the lower shelf. "Grapefruit Mist," the label said. I was tired of the Thunderbird I stashed in the pitchy evergreen yew bushes in front of the library in a paper bag. I went up to the counter.

"What's up for Halloween?" The guy had a beard.

"Oh, going to a party on campus. I'm Cool Hand Luke, in case you couldn't tell."

"I see," the man said, smiling.

I took the paper bag wrapped bottle in hand by the neck. "Thanks," I said, nodding to him.

"How 'bout some eggs," the man called after me as I left.

"Oh, no thanks. I ate fifty just yesterday," I called back, grinning as I pushed the door open into the warm leaf-strewn night.

The main campus party that night was at the AD house, overlooking the Common, not far away from the store and the town hall. I walked to her dorm, opened the door, climbed the stairs to the top floor and knocked on the door.

The door opened. She was standing there.

"Trick or treat," I said.

"Hi," she said nonchalantly.

"Hello, Princess," I said, my voice coming out husky in a way I did not try for, as if seeing her for the first time. I bit my lip, and looked down at the floor, not ready to take her in all at once.

"What should I call you?" she said, a little softer, calmer than I might have expected. She looked down, leaning back against the wall, her hips out slightly, her legs out straight, her feet balanced on her slippers.

"Cool Hand Luke. Couldn't you tell? Got my bottle of Grapefruit Mist."

Her eyebrows raised and her head tilted to the side.

"Didn't you ever see that movie? This guy keeps escaping from prison. There's this funny opening scene where he's cutting the tops off of parking meters. That's what got him into trouble in the first place. You wonder why he did it. Maybe he just felt the need to break out."

She looked forward for a moment, near the level of my chest. She kept the magazine in her hand, the door open. She was leaning on it with her back not letting it shut. She focused on something close before her, holding it close by looking down.

"Aren't you going out tonight?"

"No." She drew it out a little bit.

A small troop of girls dressed like elves came up onto the landing and knocked on the door across the hall. "Trick or treat," they yelled, not in unison, giggling as they clamored in. I looked at the Princess, smiling. She rolled her eyes.

"Halloween is for kids, don't you know."

"Oh, well, I guess it is. You have a magazine to read. What is it?"

She was reluctant to show me. I lifted it so I could see the cover.

"Just a magazine."

"Oh."

It was a woman's fashion magazine.

"And you learn something from reading them?"

"Well, yes." She opened the magazine and held it before her. "Here's an article about how the sun triggers your body clock. Seeing the sun speeds up the body's production of certain chemicals called neurotransmitters. Serotonin, for example, which helps you feel happy." She looked back down into her *Cosmopolitan*.

"Oh, yeah, I knew that," I said.

She looked up at me for a second, to check on something, to ask for something. I stood there before her, my lower lip beneath my front teeth, wanting to sway or move my shoulders.

"I like reading those magazines, too," I said softly. "Maybe you could read some to me. I like the photography."

"You have a party to go to, don't you?"

"Yeah, why don't you come? You can be a fashion model or something."

And then something quietly vibrated between us and I felt that gentle feeling of something incredibly good.

The door across the hallway opened and the elves came back out, giggling again. The kid who opened the door was a football player, an Aryan type, his head standing back on his strengthened neck. The kid noticed the Princess and I standing there with the door open. The kid stood there watching us, his neck helping him see straight.

"You could let the door close, you know. You might get tired holding it open."

"I'm okay."

I shot the football kid a glance across the hall. He stood there with his perfect tight skin. I pulled out my bottle, and looked at the kid.

"Here, would you like some?"

"No, thanks," the kid said. He got the point, though it was taking him awhile.

She leaned back against the wall, holding the door open still. She looked down, as if the magazine were open still.

"Grapefruit Mist," I said to her, imitating Bill Murray's groundskeeper from *Caddyshack*. "Very fine, very fine stuff, indeed."

"You run along to your party."

Finally the doorway across the hall closed. I stepped back a step and looked away for a moment. "Well, I'm not going to go 'til you kiss me," I said.

I stood and turned my head to the side, holding out my cheek.

"Jamie, I don't feel that way about you," she said quickly, becoming serious.

I looked down at her for a moment. "Well, then don't ever look at me ever again," I said softly.

"I... I don't look at you."

"Good. Then don't."

I turned toward the door.

"Happy Halloween."

"Bye," she said, withdrawing.

"You win, you little bastard," I thought, looking at the doorway across the hall, going back down the steps and out of the dorm.

The bottle was almost empty by the time I got to the party.

"Sorry, no townies allowed," the kid checking ID at the door said.

I ignored him and came in over the transom. A brunette girl looked at me, a smile breaking out across her face. "Don't you know him?" she said, slightly under her breath to the kid. The kid was shrugging without interest in anything as I walked past him into the noise of the party.

It was perfect, being taken for a townie. Just what Cool Hand Luke would have liked.

I grabbed a white plastic cup of beer and stood in the hallway. People passed by me in the hall without stopping, thrilled by the ingenuity of their own costumes. *Robin* stood on the staircase, two sophomore girls excited about standing below him. Taking a beer from the keg in the bathroom, a chubby redhead girl asked me who I was.

"No, you're not," she said. "I don't know who he is, anyway."

Friday I was walking to Deviancy class from the dining hall when she walked past me.

"Hi," she said, pleasantly.

"Hi," I said, letting her go on ahead.

"What you got going on this weekend?"

"My roommates are such busybodies," she said.

"Yeah," I said.

"They're throwing a party this weekend. It will probably be loud and I won't get any work done."

"Oh," I said. I let her go on ahead. I didn't feel like walking that fast in my cowboy boots.

After dinner Saturday night, Kareem and Mark dragged me along to a party at Smith. I made the mistake of running into them in the dining hall. They wanted to be wild and crazy guys, so naturally they picked me. The party was a big affair. The girls in the house knew they were quite popular. A guy in a blue blazer went by with a pipe in his teeth. "Dartmouth," I heard him say to girl in a white evening gown wearing a pearl necklace and her head leaned back and she laughed along with him. I drank a couple gin and tonics by myself in a corner. I danced with a fat girl. Then I ran.

I took the bus back by myself. I felt relieved to be going back in to Amherst. I stood in the aisle holding on to the bar above. The bus was crowded, turned to a jocular mood. I watched some UMass guys on the bus. One of them, standing in the aisle in front of me, was saying something about his mother.

"Your mother's a dirty, dirty girl," I said, using an expression I'd heard from my brother and his friends. I grinned at him, just to let him know I was kidding. The bus swung up now to the Amherst stop in front of the old library.

"Hey, come down and party with us. Come on, man," a short kid with dark curly hair said.

"Yeah, come on," another voice behind me said.

I was just about to get off the bus. I was almost to the door. I stood looking down the steps now. "Come on, man. It's going to be a great party." I looked back and they were smiling at each other. One nodded to me. What the hell. I sat back down.

The bus went down through town to the university. The bus came to the stop and we all got out. I began telling one of the quieter guys how my mother had gone to UMass, how my father had taught there awhile ago. We were walking to the high rise where the party was.

"You better get out of here," the kid said to me when no one could hear us.

"What?"

"They want to beat the crap out of you, man. Just get out of here."

It dawned on me in an uncomfortable cold-blooded kind of way. I found myself walking quickly, looking back. Now my feet were very heavy. It was going to be a long walk back, and no busses. I was plodding onward past a row of fraternity houses. An old Toyota pulled up beside me. The guy rolled down the window.

"You want a ride up to town? I'm going that way," the guy called, leaning forward holding the steering wheel. He looked at me through the open window, his mustache turned up expectantly.

He looked peaceable enough. I was dead tired.

"Where are you going?"

"Just up to four corners, to the College. Is that out of your way."

"No." The guy was looking at me now. He had glasses on, a plain look to him.

"I just like to drive around sometimes."

The guy looked over at me.

"Can I suck your cock?"

"What?"

"Can I give you head?"

"Uh, no. No, thanks, man," I said, looking forward, my arm stiffening against the car door. I felt for the handle without looking down. The car was moving along still.

"Are you sure? I'm very good at it. I know what to do," the guy said calmly. Just something to bring up.

"Really, I'm sure."

We came through the traffic light in the center of town. He kept it on through the light at the four corners, then past the turn.

"You missed the turn. Would you mind stopping?"

He drove on. "Okay. I'll turn here."

He turned to the right at the street that led to the gates of the football field.

"You sure you don't want to drive around a while?"

"No. This is fine right here."

"But your turn is back there. Let me take you up there."

"Thanks, but I'll be all right," I said, having already opened the door and gotten one foot out. He stopped the car.

I got out. I shut the door and walked quickly up a little street without looking back. It was cold out. I got to the main street. I crossed it and then I was on the lawn before the old library, feeling I was safe again.

I caught the tail end of a party at New Dorm. I was talking to a guy in my class, a wrestler. I saw her come up and stand just off my shoulder, looking over my shoulder. I was about to turn to her, but just then she turned and walked away. She went toward the dance floor, and I danced with a plain-faced girl from my class, working my way over to the Princess. When I looked for her she was gone.

I saw her as I was coming out of the dining hall. She was up ahead of me on the sidewalk, so I jogged up to her. "Go get her," Beaver, one of the guys in my class said.

"Hi," she said, looking forward, hiding a smile.

"What'ch you been up to?"

We came down the aisle and she stopped at an empty row and I followed her down it ten seats in. This far in nobody would bother us. We sat down next to each other, without a seat in between. We both put our knees up against the row in front of us. We took our notebooks out. It was nice, perhaps even nicer to have her to my left. Something was better when she was right next to me. She took her breath in and let it flow back out.

She sniffed at the sleeve of her light flannel shirt. "My roommates sprayed me with perfume," she said.

"I like yours better," I said, quietly, leaning slightly toward her.

"I don't wear perfume." She looked down.

"Oh." I bit my lip.

She opened her notebook and drew a face in along the margin of a page, a beautiful round feminine face. It hit like a punch, but in a nice way, right into me. I drew a face of my own in the margins of my blue-covered notebook. My hand moved before I could think and the face I drew was a boy's with big eyes, looking upward in loneliness. She looked down at her drawing. I peeked at it. It was quite good. Just then she scratched out her drawing. I didn't like mine so I scratched it out. Our shoulders were close, and then touching.

"That woman up there in front, she has an interesting face," she said, looking ahead at the stage.

I looked over at her sitting next to me, seeing that she was looking down toward the panel of speakers. I could only make them out as blurs.

"I can't see. I don't have my glasses with me. What does she look like?"

"Well, she's... It's her features. It's hard to describe," she said, looking back down at the notebook propped on her knees for a moment.

She was looking still, amused with something, making a study through one of her many talents.

"The kind of face that would launch a thousand ships," I asked.

"No-oh." She paused for a moment.

"I wish you could see her. She does have interesting features."

"Oh. Well, that's nice you noticed."

"Well, yes."

Then there was an enjoyable moment of awkwardness, and we looked for something else to talk about. We beamed our little talents out over the room to see what we could come up with, sitting together now, not needing to look over at each other.

"Botany," she said, drawing the word out with a slightly rising lilt, offering a sudden pronouncement. "What a stereotypically boring subject to teach," she said grandly, her chin raised gaily, in a musically British way. She looked forward over the room, a slight smile coming to the corners of her lips.

"Well, I think he's pretty cool," I said quietly. I looked down at the back of the chair before me.

It seemed to make her warm. Her lashes flickered. She sat still, surrounded by a sphere of gossipy chatter.

I remember when my father took me and a friend to see a movie playing up at the college. It had begun to snow out. He left and then Buzzy and I found out they'd cancelled the movie because of the coming storm. Buzzy's mom came and gave us a ride in a 4-wheel drive and when we turned onto Reservoir I saw our car by the side of the road, slid into the ditch. It was a long way to Ernst Road, and when we got up the hill, we were in the woods and then I saw my dad's footprints. Patiently walking all the way up in the snow. On and on, up the long road. The silence of the snowy woods, and the only show I'd ever seen from him, his quiet footsteps in the snow— you could still see them, even as powder covered them, as the woods hung over the road, keeping the wind away. One after another, up the hill.

Professor Lindsey plodded slowly up on the stage. He cleared his voice, his head moving up and down just slightly, like a bird in some sort of ritual. "Mmm, mmm," his voice sounded. He raised his hand above his head. "People," he called. The crowd quieted as soon as momentum allowed.

"We're going to talk about AIDS today," he said, and I heard him breathing us all in through his nose.

"Let's go through the ways you can be infected with the virus that causes AIDS," I heard a from the panel man say. He read off a long list. There was quiet laughter in the room, dispelling anxiety.

"I don't see what's so funny," I said under my breath.

"Yes, I don't either," she said.

The crowd drew conservative and silent.

"Can a man contract AIDS from a woman through vaginal intercourse?" asked a pimply-faced kid behind us, dark curly hair sticking out from under his Jamaican knit cap.

"Good question." The panel at the front talked back and forth, as a communal blush hovered in the auditorium.

I raised my hand. Professor Lindsey looked over the crowd, and said, "in the middle there, on the side."

"Yeah, I had a question," I said, feeling my voice carrying well. "How should we think of AIDS? Is it one particular isolated disease, or is it something big, a large family of diseases, maybe just one breed of that?"

There was off-microphone mumbling, with the panel members looking at each other.

"Uh-hrrm," said a man, clearing his voice quietly, having been picked to respond. "Well, we won't know for a long time from now, where AIDS fits in, what sort of thing it is exactly, what sort of mutation it came from. We won't know for a long time."

"Thanks." I nodded, and relaxed back in my seat.

The hour came to a close. The Princess and I walked up the aisle and left together. Then we were outside, under pines and sun, a wind far above us for birds sailing with a tip of wings across a rich blue sky.

"There was this restaurant in France where you could get anything you wanted, all the cuisine of the world," she said, a gaiety in her stride. She looked proud in her outfit.

"Like, could you get Hungarian Goulash if you wanted?"

"Yes," she said after a moment. "Exactly."

"And where is this place?"

"My parents took me to Europe when I was young."

"My parents took us to Ireland when I was a little kid," I said when she had finished. "Lousy French fries, invariably. You'd think with all those potatoes."

She laughed, lightly and easily, as people do outdoors. We came to the entrance of the dining hall ramp walking side-by-side. Then I saw Bill Richards standing directly in front of me, blocking me. I watched her continue on, now at the foot of the ramp.

Bill grabbed my hand and shook it like LaGuardia.

"Hello, Senator, how are you?"

"I'm good," I said, breaking away. "I'll catch you later, Bill."

I came up the ramp, through the doors after her. I saw her standing looking back at me, questioning my next movement. There was a distance between us now. I remembered I had a meeting with Carlson that I had not prepared for yet. I went to the men's room off to the left. When I came out she wasn't there anymore.

I walked briskly up to the Chapel. I sat down in the study lounge, looking through the notebook with the phrases carefully written out. And I thought of the expectant, half-irritated impatient look from what I saw from her without my glasses.

At the appointed time, I poked my head into Carlson's office. "Let's go get a cup of coffee at Fayerweather," he said.

We walked down past the library to the lower quadrangle. "My idea of a nightmare, coming down here for a cup of coffee just after they've closed," Carlson said as we went in through the cafeteria line.

"Just like getting to the liquor store five after ten," I said.

We sat down with our coffee at a table near a window. He pulled out the paper I'd handed him a week before, placing it before him on the table and reacquainting himself as he brought the cup to his lips.

"Your writing has improved since sophomore year," he said.

"That's actually the same paper I handed in two years ago," I said.

He waited a moment. "I hope we'll see more from you," he said. "Soon."

I looked him over for a moment, as he read from the first page again.

"So, you want to write about Hemingway the journalist. There's that selection of his pieces, *By-Line Ernest Hemingway.* You should look that up."

"It's a particular kind of journalism I was thinking about. Journalism about the guy's own life. The food he's eating, his reactions, his experiences as he has them."

"Aren't all writers journalists by that definition?"

"I suppose they are. Hemingway more so. The further he goes into the stuff of everyday, the more he has a story. He always finds a story, a novel even, just in plain life. It's like he's trying to run in one direction, telling only the raw truth, away from fiction, away from making things up, and he finds the story. And he's wise enough, I guess, to leave in the things that only matter to the story."

Carlson sipped from his coffee again, watched someone walk past behind my back then fixed his eyes back on me, as if trying not to roll them. He focused now.

"Is that a radical concept of literature," I said, shrugging. "It's not so odd. Hemingway, he treats every little detail like something sacred."

We sat silently.

"Maybe that's ultimately a religious observation, that each detail of life has meaning, that in each little thing you can read the story, like Christ knew there was a donkey waiting to take him into Jerusalem.   For Ernest Hemingway, the story is right in front of him, like the story of the two bullfighters when he goes back to Spain for the last time, an old man going back to the place of his vigor... It just goes on and on."

"What are you going to write about for our conversation here?"

"The way he writes about the textual details, life as a text, the objects, the people, the scenes, all the incidental that has meaning ultimately."

"As long as you're discussing the writing... We don't need so much of the higher truth... That's not our job here."

I was thinking about the Princess, the way she looked at me, saying there should be another beat after meeting and sitting together in Deviancy class. I'd seen it without my glasses, blurry. I felt it, how there was another vibration out there, another back and forth, one that would lead to another one, and then another. I swallowed now, and there was something stuck in my throat. All we needed was just to meet in some easy way that was not intimidating and things would find their own way. I felt it now over the whole front of my body, the connection, the magnetic draw.

Life comes at you in waves, vibrating, when it is real, when you are alive to something. That power is why one has to take a nap sometimes, all of it coming through you, running through every atom in your body.

I looked back at Carlson now, selfish, typical, self-concerned, a kind of black hole, and I sat there, thinking of my girl and how I had missed something. For what?

I wished I was laying on my side, next to her with my arm over her, as the world spun slowly with us at the very center of it all.

My father came out later that afternoon and we drove up to Maine. We stayed up at a motel on the spit of land leading out to Bailey's Island, about to close for the season. We ate quietly at a seafood restaurant. I had a piece of fish. The car windows were fogged with the cold when we came out.

The Red Sox were playing in the Championship Series for the American League Title. We watched the last innings of the game on the television in the room.

"Let's go down to the water," my dad said.

We drove back up the road to the Giant's Staircase, not passing a single car. We walked down the step-like stone formation to the edge of the water. I followed him in the moonlight, watching his heavy woolen outer shirt descend through the low scrub pines, his hair catching the silver of the stars. The pines stuck up at us, their arms swaying quietly, almost silently in the wind, and I couldn't see anything below us through them in the dark, just hearing the surf somewhere below.

Boom, the surf came in, then sloshing in rocky throats, then hissing back out, the land having taken just the exact energy of it out so that it would come back.

Then the land came to an end, laid bare, the granite strata tilted upward, the path ending on a large horizontal slab. The sea down below us came rushing on with each wave, swirling through all the cracks it could reach, covering the lower flat rock, pouring back out, sweeping back in again differently. The stars were brilliant in the clear sky, the Milky Way stretching all the way across the black. I had never seen as many.

"Magnificent," my dad said.

"You want to hold on to them all."

The waves came in, the surf rolling unstoppable into the cove below us, the sea foam curling over the black rocks then hissing back out with a strange quiet. It was late at night, just the two of us standing there underneath all the laid-out wisdom of the stars. The rocky point dropped down at an angle to meet the agile sea.

We drove back to the motel, the silent pines towering darkly above the winding road that rose and fell, twisted and turned. Then the road was flat and the bark of the trunks shone in the light of the headlamps, as if each were caught by surprise.

The motel was silent when we pulled in off the road, the lot before the low building empty except for one Ford pick-up truck. Dad put the key in and the door creaked open. In bed I pulled the thin blanket over me. I felt very tired, but I wanted to talk with her. I lay there what seemed a long time, as I was cold still, and then I guess I fell asleep.

On the way back down the coast before we stopped at a gift shop in York. I picked out a small red stuffed lobster doll. We had lobster rolls from a shack at the end of a walkway above a salt marsh, the sea in the distance beyond the grasses. Then we got on the highway, as if to undo it all almost, all the piney quiet and the sea air further and further behind us on smaller roads.

It was a warm sunny Sunday afternoon when we got back. A slender freshman girl smiled at us perkily from across the intersection of four corners at the middle of town. We sat down for an early dinner by a window on the main drag. He ordered in French, without batting an eye. I felt impatient as we ate.

I regretted I had been so when my father was back on road heading home. He had difficulty with the glare driving at night.

I called her up from the black campus phone on the wall outside my room that night.

"This phone has a very long cord and I can go down the back steps and walk around outside."

"Oh," she said.

"Oh, hi, Mr. Squirrel. Good to see you."

There was a pause on her end of the line. "Go inside," she said.

"Okay. I was up in Maine with my dad."

"Oh."

"I got..." I started to say.

"I have to go," she said. "Bye," she said before I could continue.

"Okay. Bye," I said quietly.

She had hung up the receiver. I stood there, outside the door.

I was about to send her the cute furry red little lobster doll through the campus mail. I wanted to. I went back in to my room and it sat there beneath the light on my desk and I began to feel sore. She had shut something off, that next vibration due, when I had offered again after suffering to start it again for so long in a way she didn't know. And so I had to go back to suffering, in hopes of a little touch of a finger that said it was okay. "It wasn't my fault, it wasn't my fault," I wanted to say, but then maybe it was, and what did I have to do with a dry ponderous thesis anyway.

The next weekend it was Parent's Weekend and my father was coming out again. I took the janitor's mop bucket and filled it with ice and put a bottle of Wild Turkey down in it, carrying it with me to the party at AD. An Asian girl stayed the night in my room. She asked me in the morning if I had a condom, but I didn't and so we didn't do anything. I didn't feel like it anyway.

My dad and I went to lunch down at the Parent's Luncheon in the new gym, folding tables laid out with table clothes. We got our plates. I looked around over the heads of people. The room was bright and murmuring noisily. We walked around carefully a little bit, and ended up sitting with a girl named Hope who called my name out when we were right in front of her table. She was from Tennessee. Her father was a minister, but plain-clothes and very laid-back, and with a good chuckle. The girl knew I wanted to be a writer some day. I looked around. I did not see any sign of the Princess.

We drove down to South Amherst to visit with old family friends the Gregorians. I watched the two Siamese chase their tails in circles. I was looking out the sliding glass doors over the garden when I decided that I was going to be sick. I got up and went slowly to the bathroom and threw up quietly into the toilet. They looked up at me when I came back into the sitting room.

"Are you okay?" Mrs. Gregorian asked.

"I had to throw up," I said. "Sorry."

"Something must have disagreed with you," my father said.

"Too much poison from last night."

We walked down by the football game, then drove into Northampton for a look around. When we got back to my room there was a poster still in plastic rolled up in front of my door. There wasn't any note attached. I picked it up and took it out of its plastic. It was a life-sized poster of James Dean, the cigarette-holding pose from *Rebel Without A Cause*. There were adhesive tabs stuck on each corner, and while I noticed them I did not pay particular attention to them. I thought it was the girl I had spent the night with who had brought it. She knew I liked James Dean.

We were going up to the Deerfield Inn to meet Martinez and Bill Richards and their parents. There was something hard-nosed, businesslike about Bill's academic mother and father. They looked around as if they would have preferred another table. Martinez's old man, sitting in the dim light, hardly looked at his son. I felt sorry for involving my father, who seemed uncharacteristically puzzled, disappointment in his face, boredom in his reactions, and I thought maybe he had something to say about who or what sort of situation we should be dining in. Something was missing, I thought. We should have been somewhere else. And I had failed, having gone along with something agreeably rather than planning anything out carefully as I should have, so as to introduce my special old father to someone special to me.

There was a party back at the house and I was watching as the Red Sox lost, which didn't make me too happy either. By that point I was feeling pretty goddamn irritated. I went upstairs, changed, came down and then I was talking to two tall girls, juniors who seemed odd and interesting and attractive all at the same time. I was talking some talk with them when I saw Jessica Dorfmann in profile in the main hallway as I came down the stairs. Later on, Rick, her math tutor, came up to me.

"So did you see who's here?"

"Yeah, I saw who's here."

"She said she's a bit tipsy," Rick said.

"Oh, that's nice." I thought for a moment how I wanted to show her my room. I wanted to play guitar for her. Give her the lobster doll in my room. "I thought Miss Morality didn't like to drink." The irritations, the out-of-place and not-at-the-right-time quality of everything, seemed to be increasing by the moment, such that I almost ran out. And most of all, I felt mad at her for hanging up on me, like she shouldn't have done that and so I was mad at her and couldn't speak to her.

On one side of the room I saw her standing there. I looked at the two tall junior girls standing near me, looking me over. "No, she's not here except as some sort of trick," I thought. I was talking again now with the two girls. I took them both out on the dance floor. I saw the Princess standing by the opening to the dance floor, looking over at me. She looked slender and vulnerable, and I ignored her. I let her stand there, and I couldn't see the apology in her quiet glance over at me as she stood there alone, her hands behind her back holding the door frame.

By now the beer buzz was kicking in. I decided I liked the dark haired one of the tall girls. She'd taken care of birds of prey the summer before. I walked her back to her dorm and we went together up to her room. She lit a candle. After awhile she pulled me back up to her. "I broke my back once," she whispered to me. "I think there was some nerve damage."

I woke up in her room. She was asleep still. I went to the dining hall early. I felt like hell.

It might have occurred to me as I ate my breakfast, sipped my coffee there by the window, looking out at the rain, a cold one, that was pouring down. The Princess had come to my door, even with her parents, laying the poster down on the floor, having carefully put four stickers on the back, one at each corner, so the poster wouldn't fall. And then she had come to the house where I lived, far away from campus, up on a hill, on Parent's Weekend, and I had fucked it all up.

I saw the Princess at the next Deviancy class. It was frigidly cold out. We were getting our papers back. The professor stood up on the stage. "The newspaper accounts have created a deviant, um, um," he grunted with nasal proclamation, raising his beak.

I heard her name called to come get her paper. I could see over the crowd, the cold look on her face. She turned away as she went back to her seat.

CHAPTER SIX

I carried my books back from the library and headed down to Thursday Night Tap at AD. The snow angled down beneath the street lamps, covering the higher parts of the common. My hiking boots crunched softly on the snow. I came up the steps and past the pillars.

There was a card game down in the taproom. I took my beer and went back up to the parlor, the steady powdery stream outside the windows. The fireplace was empty. "*Two dozen other stupid reasons*," I sang with the *English Beat* song playing on a boombox, "*Why we should suffer for this...*"

I got my Dad's old cashmere overcoat from the sofa and went back outside into the snow. I stood at the crossroads beneath the traffic lights. The glittering powder lay clean across the road. I walked up past the library. I stood in the middle of the quad, the snowflakes falling wet and silent down through the oaks, the lights of the freshman dorms warm and quiet. I walked down the field to the Social Dorms.

The Princess's dorm stood at the edge of the woods, her suite three floors up. Her room faced out over the railroad tracks. I'd been by once in the fall. I'd stood in the common room and then she turned and walked down the steps without saying anything. I stood there, and then I left.

I launched a snowball up to the dark window on the third floor. It went up through the clean air. The whole backside of the building was dark. The snowball hit the wall above the window, disintegrating silently against the brick. I tossed another one just a little wide. The third one landed on the window with a light whunk. I threw another one, and then another.

I saw the shade being pulled down. "That's no fun," I said to myself. I went in through the basement door and up the stairs. I knocked on the door of the suite. The door opened a crack. A boyish little girl stood looking up at me, her dirty blond hair short, her brown eyes like shiny little buttons.

"Cops are after me," I said hoarsely. "You gotta' hide me." I let my eyes run over the floor on both sides of where we were standing. I looked beyond her through the opening in the door. The light was on in the main room.

"The cops aren't after you," she said slowly, not taking her eyes away, a smile peeking out. She looked at me very straight, studying me.

"They're not?" I said, ducking my head down slightly.

"No."

"Are you sure?" I twitched. I looked down into her eyes.

"Yes, I'm sure," she said.

"Positive?"

"Positive," she pronounced. Her little chin made a pleasant little nod.

"Um, okay." I let my brow drop. I looked a little bit behind me, over my shoulder. She kept her easy hold on the edge of the door, letting it swing just slightly.

I gave her a quick wink, turned and bounded off, down the steps out the front, back outside. The snow blanketed the grass. I walked across it rather than staying on the path. It was cold and I had a ways to walk now. I was hungry all of a sudden. I was happily numb to the cold, and I felt like singing.

I called the Princess the next day from the library in the afternoon. Her roommate answered, and then she came to the phone.

"Hello?" she said.

"Hi."

Silence.

"It's Jamie."

"Was that you last night?" she demanded abruptly.

"Umm..."

"That was you!" she yelled, her voice suddenly high and sharp. "We thought some crazy man was attacking us!"

My stomach sank.

"But I was just throwing..."

"That wasn't even my window!"

"Oh."

"It's Laura's. Do you know how long you stood there?"

"No, not exactly."

"You stood out there for fifteen minutes without stopping. Fifteen... minutes."

"That's an exaggeration," I said.

"We were ready to call the Police."

"Oh, come on," I said, quietly.

"We were going to call the Police!"

"I'm not some axe-murderer," I said.

"Why do you do such things anyway?" she shouted, cutting me off.

"I just wanted to talk to you." I'd been outplayed, yet again.

"You must never speak to me ever again, do you hear me?" she said, loudly and with paced evenness.

"Okay," I said.

"Hi, and hi back," she went on, rapidly, "in the dining hall, if we run into each other, but that's it. Only if we can't avoid it."

I didn't say anything.

"Do you understand?" she said, not losing momentum.

"Yeah," my voice cracked. "Hi, hi."

"You're going to leave me alone," she said, her voice rising again.

"Right," I said.

"How can I tell you so you'll understand?"

"Okay. I understand."

She didn't say anything.

"Bye."

"Bye," she declared, as if she would hold me to it.

I put the phone down and went back to the desk. I sat down, looking out the window. The snow of the night held on the shaded sides of houses and yards. I sat there for an hour or so. Maybe there was some poem about snow on the dark side of houses, on the side that doesn't get the sun, and how it feels neglected and the snow is white, as if to cheer up that part of things. I was looking down at the roof of one of the Dickinson houses far in the distance in a grove of pines. "Ahh, that's it. 'Success is counted sweetest by those who ne'er succeed. To comprehend a nectar requirest sorest need.'"

That night, I sat with my tray in front of me toward the back of the dining room, picking at my mashed potatoes and gravy. She came out of the line with her tray, wearing a fatigue jacket. Her hair shone, full-bodied and straight. She lingered by the salad bar. She looked over at the back table where I was sitting. I looked down at my plate again. My eyes hurt. It was like all year I had just wanted one person to be nice to me, one person to defend me, understand me, and there were many voices going on in the room but no one was saying anything that could bring me comfort. She seemed to shine in the dim light, and I felt her motion as I looked away and hid under my brow.

When I left she was standing in the foyer between the door and me. Two girls talking to each other moved into my way. I swung right and the Princess stepped sideways with her long legs into my path, drawing herself up tall, blocking me. She had her head down, a playful look rising across her face. I felt the presence of her body, upright as she drew a breath in. I stepped toward her, moving faster now, not looking up. I went past her. Her eyes turned to study me. But I could not look up, or betray something far too personal. Maybe that was why she was torturing me, to see when I'd break.

A space to the side of her opened. I slipped around her to the door, seeing it before me. I pushed against it. The dark bulk swung open and then it shut behind me and the noise of inside, all the busy murmuring about nothing, endless, was gone, and I was standing by some overgrown yew bushes. I shoved my hands deep in my pockets and walked up the silent street, holding my dad's overcoat about me. I walked and walked and then I was at the bottom of the hill and still had to go up it. I stopped and stood there, looked up for a moment. I turned around and looked back, and then I went up the hill and didn't want to go out the rest of the night. I played my guitar.

There was a special dinner that week, a certain collection of dorms invited along with faculty advisors. The Deme Dinner, as it was called, the first of its kind, was an attempt on the part of college administration to adjust campus social life in the wake of the passing of fraternities. I found my way to the line that had formed at the entrance. My thesis advisor Professor Carlson stood right in front of me. I was too tired to avoid him.

"Mr. Tarnowski," the man said, turning halfway around stiffly. "I've been meaning to talk with you. You haven't handed in any work since we talked."

"No, sir, I haven't."

"The hour is getting late. We need to see some writing from you."

"I'm working on it," I said.

"The ball is in your court now," Carlson said, looking straight from under his brow up at me, standing still, as if he were trying not to shake his head at me. He turned and moved on toward a group of African American students, leaning forward to receive an embrace from a short girl with braces.

I stood there, and somehow from behind me I felt some gentle vibe of someone getting how I might have felt, some appreciation of my being defenseless but standing my ground in some form of bravery. I took a glance back over my shoulder. The Princess stood there, looking down at the shined floor. Her roommate, a silk scarf tied around her white turtleneck, looked straightly at me for a moment, clearly, as if to check on something. I turned back around forward. "Well, here I am," I thought.

I stepped through the doorway into Annex itself, the tables spread with white table clothes. An ice sculptor of a swan glistened on the main table in front, rising above decorative cabbages placed on green felt, below which, on silvery trays, sat large wedges and blocks and rounds of hard cheeses, yellow and white, like buildings of a tiny city.

I passed the swan and made my way across the room. Gould and Rosenstern, roommates from sophomore year, called from a front table on the far side of the room. "Come sit with us," Rosenstern said. "Dove's coming."

I sat along the wall facing away from the podium, set up in front of the salad bar.

"What all this about," Gould said, leaning against Rosenstern.

"This is our new social life," Rosenstern said.

"What's the podium for?" Gould asked.

"We're going to get up and tell everyone about the time we changed the lettering on the sign at the movie theater on Route Nine. 'The Doof's Penis.'"

Dove sat down.

"You should have brought that rooster." They had planted one in someone's room once.

Far ahead of me, four tables away, I saw her sit down. I ducked my head down slightly, and pressed my lips together, turning away and then I looked back. She sat opposite, facing me with no one seated in between. I looked back down at my silverware, unfolding the napkin in my lap. The Dean of Students, his hair combed over, rose to the podium, looking up into the air. She looked up. No one had come to sit in between.

I put my left hand out on the table, let it rest there, open and gentle, full of touch and a strange energy coming out of it. I let my fingers spread out, my palm against the table, then rising again, so alive and balanced a thing, such a miracle of dexterity, blood running through it.

"Amherst thrives on its one to one relationships," the Dean began.

The Dean looked out over us, as if turning a page. He welcomed Cormorant, Professor of American History, to the podium. The Dean fixed the microphone for him with a focused grin, the sound of the bending gooseneck creaking over the P.A. system.

I leaned forward, looking down at the table again, listening to the little old man's high voice carry. I bit my lip.

Student workers, dressed in white pressed shirts and black slacks, delivered salads to the tables.

"De Tocqueville observed an America where an interesting experiment was taking place. He observed people of all classes together, rubbing elbows, nobleman and commoner. He got a big kick out of it." A server placed a salad before her. The little white-haired man raised his voice again, strands of his white hair about to fall back down across his forehead. "The clever Frenchman had a great interest in this new land and he wished the best for it," he said firmly, looking out over his audience. "Amongst his principle worries--and the one that bothered him most, with prescience quite particular to his commentary--was the foresight of a tyranny of the majority."

I thought of how she had come to sit there. It was probably a coincidence, just a free table in a quiet corner of the room. I kept turning back to watch to the historian, strands of his white hair about to fall back down across his forehead but staying somehow in line.

"De Tocqueville diagnosed the matters of our situation long before we could have even imagined such a threat," the little man pronounced, his chin raised in a mighty way. "Other nations, as we well know, have had their struggles with the social infirmities that come with a political system conceived in the ideal. Upon the heels of Marxist principles, came the Soviet Totalitarianism that flourished so terribly under Joseph Stalin. The intellectual, the artist, the dissenter, disappeared."

I looked back at her again. She had turned to her friend sitting across from her, her hands placed in her lap. The girl sitting next to her turned to her and they made eye contact without saying anything.

"The good news is that thanks to the wisdom of the Founding Fathers, Democracy in American has been healthy so far," piped the little old man, a strand of white hair sticking up. The Dean rose instantly and shook hands with the historian.

"Past his bedtime," Gould said, leaning over to me, and I nodded, smiling.

Salad plates were cleared.

Then the dinner plates were brought forward. Dinner arrived at our table, chicken breast, stuffed with wild rice and mushroom, parsley and a slice of orange on a leaf of curly lettuce as a garnish. "Not bad," Dove said, grinning.

"They must want more money out of us," Gould said. I watched her look down, her knife and fork in her hands. She put the fork to her mouth. I bit my lip.

Duchamp came to the podium.

I looked down at the table. She looked down at the table before her. I looked down obediently at my plate for a moment, then back at her as she turned toward Duchamp. Then she looked down again.

"The scene is wintertime and Ivan, the middle of the Karamazov brothers, a questioning atheist of the rationalist sort--you know the type--has beaten a drunken peasant unlucky enough to fall into his path..."

Ivan came back and picked up the peasant and took him to an inn. And then schoolboys were throwing rocks at each other. Then something about this youngest brother Alyosha, and precocious child named Kolya.

I looked down at the table again, the candles lit, and the two of us, facing each other, as if we were at the same table. I put my hand on the table and imagined her hand being there.

"Alyosha, has brought the schoolboys together." Our plates were clean now and the room was silent. "They have all gathered at the boy's bedside. The dog jumps up on the bed, licking him in the face. 'Zutchka,' the boy cries. At the deathbed, the schoolboys standing..."

The candlelight flickered and I felt her sitting there.

"The simple 'Hurrah for Karamazov,' from the boys, at the end," the man said, his voice thickening, "brings us a moment. Our participation is equal to our presence. The boys are thinking of their own achievement, and yet they are also to enjoy a sense of displacement, of visitation. And we can imagine, the young man who has seen this terrible drama unfold so painfully in his family, with all parties asking and deserving sympathy, Dimitri brought to the same recognition by a stranger placing a pillow under him as he sleeps in the courtroom, we can imagine this young man, inhabiting, as if from a distance, a freedom from the illusion of self. And for a moment being able to pass it to his little flock, his fellows, seeing it in them. That is one moment of education. Alyosha is awake, an artist, for his work, and the schoolboys are with him there, in this quiet scene that comes at the end of this long, strange mystery, that brings it all together."

I watched him turn his head away. There was silence and then applause. He stood for a moment and then his tall figure slipped away in long strides. Dessert was served. There was more clicking of silverware and plates, jokes back and forth, and smiles over coffee and tea. The lights went up.

I stood up at the drink dispensers at the front and poured myself a glass of milk. The Princess came forward, her friends imitating her expression as they followed in her footsteps. I turned and faced her as she came forward. She went past me, looking off in the distance like there was a horizon.

Maybe I was about to say something. Maybe I was just about to say hi. But I let her go past me. I held the short bubbleglass in my hand. I walked slowly to the coat racks. I heard a bit of laughter far up ahead.

I was the poet of the town. No one knew it. Maybe they thought I was even the idiot, but that was okay. You didn't have to go and announce it anyway. It was just something you had in your soul. That was where words came from anyway. Maybe it was from your mom showing you Emily Dickinson's grave, behind a shop on the main strip. What mattered was that you cared enough to lose yourself and become other people. And that was the only way, because it protected you from things you couldn't take anyway, all that didn't mean anything.

Duchamp knew it somehow, if he wasn't an active poet himself. He'd passed that on, knowing he'd help one come to be, if that was all he ever did. There were simply physic laws regarding poets. You just needed someone to be as he was meant to be, just letting him be, as he would be. That was a fine thing to learn, and maybe you couldn't learn it until you were completely defeated, so as to lose some part of yourself.

Maybe it's a hard thing for another to see in someone, as if then one too is called upon to be.

I took the bus home for Thanksgiving break. There was a dim light above my head, blackness outside the windows, the steady roar of the motor underneath calling out for something in the empty air.

My mom picked me up at the bus station. I saw her waiting outside as the bus rolled up to the curb. She looked around expectantly, shifting her feet as looked up then sideways over at the front of the bus. She couldn't see me through the tinted window. I looked down and saw her looking toward the door, her sweet poetic lonesomeness, her bright energy, her short lithe frame of endurance. I wanted to cry almost, but I picked my bag up from the seat of the dead-aired bus interior and walked toward the front when it was my turn, toward the low glowing dashboard lights, then turning to go down the runway of the stairs. I went out and she saw me and her hair was short above her face and no one so pure as my mom.

She had an excited smile about her that she had dearly earned. She'd probably been close to giving up, would be a guess of mine. She had found a collection of letters in the rare book room of the Syracuse University Library. Bright and awake, she told me a little bit about them and a little of what they meant about women's literacy.

"That's wonderful," I said. I drove up the dark road, smiling and happy and there would be a sandwich and good sleep there even as it was. Tinkerbell would be there.

My poor sweet beautiful mom, brave little thing, and no one to take care of her, just me and her driving up the road, the night city barren and cold, our jackets on in the car, the heater on, on to the apartment where she lived.

My brother came from Boston and on Thanksgiving Day we went to zoo. We walked past the lions, lounging behind glass in their quarters, the mix of tiny monkeys in their own little habitat, green and warm, next to the chimps. The gorilla sat stooped over, licking up vomit on the cement ground before him. The elephants were outside. The day was mild and one of them kept swinging his hindquarters back and forth, developing a ponderous erection, feeling his oats, his own rhythm in the low winter sun. We had a good chuckle and the elephant kept swaying. "Good for you, Mr. Elephant," my brother's look seem to say and I smiled up at him again.

We took the circuitous walk past the wolf pen, the deer hiding in the woods, the bobcats, and the bear, stirring out of his cave, bent over at something. I watched each animal carefully, pondering their limbs, the motions with which they conducted their animal business. I watched the wolf trot on light paws back and forth, back and forth very patiently along the steel bar and chain link fence, looking for a way out, looking for a way out. Each time he came to the end of the fence he turned around in the same automatic way, turning his neck with the same rhythm each time, his legs following underneath him, springing on his paws, like slowly beating a drum.

At the end of the vacation I took the bus back to Amherst, practicing telling the story of the little cowboy and his invisible friend the bear. I looked out the tinted windows at the rolling thruway landscape. I wasn't good at telling stories, and I wanted to tell her the story. I called her the next day, after I got back. I wanted to tell her the story of the little cowboy and the big bear and the ending I'd made up for them. It seemed like time for a fresh start.

"Hi," she said, curtly when she answered the phone.

"How was your break?"

"Okay."

There was a pause on her end.

"I missed the shit out of you," I said, relieved to hear her voice again. It seemed to express a little bit of how I felt, like I was a tree full of water about to be tapped.

"You missed the shit out of me," she said, slowly, word by word.

"Yes." It was one of those things you can't control. I was full of monkeys and bears and wolves and elephants and all sorts of creatures that wanted to call out.

"Oh," she said, backing away from the phone, holding it out at arm's length by the sound of it. I could hear her anger, at the inappropriateness that was me.

"Look, I know that's not a good way to put it, but it's true."

"How could you say such a thing?" she shouted. "God."

"That's not how I meant to say..."

"No! That's not what anyone would say," she said bitterly, enunciating each word like a small blow upon a hand.

"I guess not."

"Why can't you just be normal? I'm not interested in you. Can't you get it? Why do you keep bothering me?"

"Uh, I... I thought you were just being difficult."

"Oh!" Her voice backed away again from the phone. "You admit it! You thought I was just being difficult," she said loudly, adding another huff, before coming back to hit again.

"I was just being honest."

"You're a sadomasochist! That's what you are, a sadomasochist."

There was a pause, while more wind gathered in her sails to find another tack.

"I approve of everything you do," I said, not far above a whisper.

She didn't say anything.

"I'm just trying to be myself. I know I sound crazy sometimes. I can't help it."

She held the line, in remarkable silence and stillness.

"They were just white. No color," I said. Maybe she'd been about to say something, but that held her off, remembering the box of roses I'd brought her before.

"I approve of everything you do. Even this."

Silence came over the phone.

"I'd do anything for you," I said, feeling a strange depth to my voice like I had a cold. I hadn't meant to say it. I didn't want it to be fake or too early. It had come out. "You're like my hero, or something."

Then she didn't say anything again.

And then I said, "Oh, forget it," as if something were catching up to me. I tried to think of something else to say, but then I said, "Bye," the air flowing out of me.

And she said, "bye." Gently, as then it had ended, in a way that sounded understanding.

Then I put the phone back on the hook gently and went back into my room and lied back on the bed without any lights on, just laying there, thinking about everything, as people do sometimes.

Close to the end, I took a walk down by the football field. I came back up the hill. The grass was hard on the bare terraced grass slope. I found myself standing in front of the Chapel, the bright white pillars lit by raised floodlights. Voices sang from within, reverberating off the bricks of the two old dorm buildings to each side.

A small sign on the door announced the Vespers Concert. I came up the flight of worn stone steps hearing the music and the singing came down toward me. I slipped quietly past an older couple into a spot in the corner in the last pew. I hadn't shaved. I didn't have my glasses on. I kept my army jacket on.

The figures on stage were singing, "*Oh Little Town of Bethlehem*," the music swelling over the crowd, faces shining in the bright light. "Lamb of God," the voices sang, crossing over each other, fugue-like.

Then people were standing, moving forward. I went out the back door, ahead of the older couple. I turned and stood at the bottom of the steps. They passed without looking at me. I walked down toward the dining hall. The crowd was talking out front of the Chapel, everyone smiling.

I found Gould and Rosenstern in Annex, sitting at a front table. I was chewing on my salad when she sat down with her friends at the table next to ours.

"How's your novel coming?" Gould said aloud so they could hear it.

"Oh, I've put it on the shelf for awhile. Letting it marinate I guess." I cut a Swedish meatball in half with the side of my fork.

I walked back to my room and started packing for Christmas break. I called her from the black phone on the wall outside my door.

"Hello." It was the roommate.

"Hi, may I speak to Jessica please."

"One moment," she said.

"Hello?" It was her voice, high and clear.

"Hi, it's Jamie."

"Oh, hi," she said.

"Uhm, I just wanted to wish you a Merry Christmas," I said. My voice was a whole lot rougher than I had planned. Maybe I was getting a cold.

"Thank you," she said happily. "Merry Christmas to you, too."

"Thanks," I said, my voice about to crack. "Well, I mean it."

"Yes," she said.

I turned from the phone on the wall outside my door to look out the open door. Just then big light flakes of snow began twirling down before the dark hemlocks behind the house.

"Oh, look," I said. "It's starting to snow out."

"Is it? How nice," she said.

"Well," I said, my voice getting rough again, "okay. I'll let you go."

"Bye."

"Bye."

I put the phone back down and looked out at the open doorway into the darkness. The snow had stopped.

I took the bus home for Christmas break. Christmas Eve, after we read Dylan Thomas aloud, *It's a Wonderful Life* came on.

"Discouraged," my brother said, repeating what the angel said about George Bailey's predicament. "That's so perfect."

I watched George Bailey go down to the bar. I watched him talking into the back of his hand as he drank, wiping his mouth. I had to crouch at the foot of my mom's bed to watch.

Then later on George Bailey was back on the bridge and the snow starts falling again. I filled up.

Later we all went to bed. I lay down on my stomach under the blankets and hugged the pillow in my arms, resting my head on it, pretending, wishing it were her.

When I woke on Christmas morning the tree had fallen slightly to the side. Mom and I fixed it, retying the fishing line that held it in place. I mumbled something.

"Don't swear. It's Christmas," my mom said. My brother was still sleeping.

The plastic we had put up on the windows was holding well enough, the winter light out on the street opaque through it.

I went for a drive up to the old road after the holiday visits were over. I stopped by the low snowbank cut by the plow at the top of the first rise, at the bottom of the road, the road narrowing beyond as it climbed into the woods. I got out and stood and looked over the frozen reservoir. I went down and through the opening along the concrete dam. Ice had caught the bent cattail husks. I walked out on the ice, shuffling my feet forward across a dusting of snow.

I lay down on my back on the ice. I looked up at the sky, gray from end to end, moving onward, unchanging.

There had been a great blue heron that came in the summertime to the reservoir. I'd get up early in the morning and bicycle down the road with my father's camera to try to capture it on film. I'd wait patiently by the edge of a grassy point, the blue-bodied dragonflies buzzing in and out over the bank as the sun grew warm, the water beginning to smell awake in its own dark green algae way. The bird would appear suddenly, taking off low over the green water, its wings beating by some slow prehistoric method of flight. I snapped once or twice a few hasty pictures of the bird from a distance against the sky, coming in over the trees at the far end of the water, a few of it taking to flight from the cove, but the photos never did justice to the bird or to the way it flew or to the color of its feather. We wondered what a bird like that was doing so far north, but there it was each summer, standing on long legs atop of the dam. I never got a good picture of it, but it was enough that it came to our little reservoir.

We'd see the heron from the car, my mom and I. If she saw it by herself, she always told me about it later.

CHAPTER SEVEN

When I got back I walked up to the Chapel to look at the list, a piece of paper on the bulletin board of the department chair, names typed out in two columns. A list. One was a girl who wouldn't kiss me when I stood in her doorway one night. The quiet guy doing Kerouac had grown a beard. Never had a lot to say. I'd never seen him drink a beer once. My name wasn't on the list.

I stepped out the door and looked over the quadrangle. The cold air was thick, heavy like water.

I went to the library to write the Princess a letter, just to get things straightened out in my own head as much as anything else. I worked on it in the afternoon at the library, looking out the window now and then, 'til it was dark out. I was standing in line in the dining hall minding my own business when I saw her come up the spiral staircase with two of her girlfriends.

"Oh, fuck," I said, under my breath, but it came out loud enough, lip-readable.

She stood still for a second at the top of the stairs, looking down at the floor, so that her friends would lead. The two girlfriends led her away behind me toward the middle of the three upstairs dining halls.

"What the hell is she doing back," I said to myself.

"Hey, I got *Green Hills of Africa* for you."

I turned around. Junior guy from Ohio, long hair. Good kid. Peale.

"Thanks."

"I got it in my bag. Out in the hall."

It took a moment to register. I looked at him.

"Okay."

So I left the line and followed the kid with long hair back down the hall, passing the line where she was standing.

She stood there at the end of the line, her head down.

I followed the guy to the shelves in the entryway. Peale reached into his bag and pulled out a green-covered paperback.

"Thanks a lot, man," I said.

"Yeah, it's supposed to have some good parts about writing. Yeah, the dude liked hunting," Peale said, smiling, shifting his weight to his other foot and brushing his long hair back to the side of his head.

"You can keep it man, I don't need it," Peale said.

"No, I'll just... I'll be done with it by the end of the month."

"No, keep it."

I nodded. "Thanks," I said.

I passed by her again as I walked back to the line. She looked down at her feet as I came by.

Later that week I went by the Office of Career Counseling. She was sitting at the end of a big table in the room of brochures. I came in and sat down in the open chair next to her. I looked around the room at the different people there, Jones, with his hair wet from lacrosse practice in his puffy down coat.

"Hi," she said, looking forward at the papers before her.

"What are you doing back?"

"I thought I'd look for some summer internships. Do something beneficial in the world," the Princess said, lifting her voice a tone above her normal register.

I looked over, craning slightly down at her collection of folders and stapled papers. "Uh-huh."

She wrote something down carefully in her wire-bound notebook.

I glanced over the table, at the papers, folders and pamphlets before everyone. "I thought I was going to be working on my thesis but they cut me," I said.

She looked down at her stack of folders, eyes open slightly wider.

I shrugged. "Oh well. Wasn't cut out for it, I guess."

She looked down, closer to herself.

"So, what are these organizations you're looking at?"

"Many are in Washington. Nonprofits," she said.

I turned away from her and looked around the room. She looked down, engaged in her papers. "This one is dedicated to the elimination of nuclear weapons."

"Oh," I said. "That's cool."

I scratched my head. I had it in my mind that I was going to go home and write something.

"Uh, I got to get going," I said.

"Okay," she said, tilting her head just slightly away from me, gently.

I stood and walked out of the room. I stopped to glance at a newspaper, and some guy I knew came up to talk to me about banking jobs. A quiet poetic girl from my class came out and patted me on the side of my arm below my shoulder. "See you later, Jamie," she said, her look strangely full, quite unlike herself, I thought.

I got back to my room. I was going to write like Ernest Hemingway. I pulled out a piece of paper. I ended up not writing anything.

The next week of the January term I went to a hockey game. I kept warm in my walks by wearing layers, a sweater, Ike jacket, a barn coat on top. I came in to the arena and sat down next to Vincent. She was sitting up a row to my right.

"So what do the lines mean?" Vincent asked. "I've never understood that."

"You can't put your player across that front line toward the goalie there before the puck crosses it. That way you can't have someone up waiting by the goalie before the puck even gets up there. And if you're back defending, you can't shoot the puck all the way back across the three lines, just to get rid of it. That's called icing."

"That's cold."

"It lets you get reorganized, I guess. The referee brings the puck back all the way and there's a face off." I had my hands in my pockets, leaning comfortably back against the bench row behind.

"What's a face off? It sounds bad."

"The man with the stripes gets everyone to stand still and drops the puck into play. You know, when the two guys slap at the puck with their sticks?"

"Yes, I've seen that. How do you know all this?"

"This is what they do in my hometown on a Saturday night."

Vincent got up and left. I glanced over at her, her face bathed in the light reflected off the ice as she looked out over the scene.

I slid up one bench, now on the same bench where she was sitting, with no one in between. She had an open look on her face as she looked out over the ice as the lines were changed, a willingness to smile. She turned to her friend Daria, leaning agreeably over to her, not saying anything, looking down then up.

I sat for another moment with my hands beside me resting on the bench. I got ready to slide over toward her across the empty space.

Three underclassmen came along. I hadn't see them coming until they were climbing up the bleacher rows toward the open space between us. They were freshmen.

"There's a party down at B-Dorm," I said, loud enough so she would hear. The final buzzer sounded. She got up quickly and left, disappearing through the crowd in the brightly lit foyer.

I went down to B-Dorm. My buddies. I didn't have anything to say. I looked out the window and saw her walking across the icy field below the art museum with the two tall sophomores from the basketball team. They walked across the slope thirty yards away to the entrance to the dorm just up the hill, the old chemistry building. The guys swaggered forward, hands in their lettermen jackets. She lagged behind slightly. She looked down as she followed them in. I looked at my watch. It was past one.

Walking home along a back street I stopped. The moon was in the sky behind a light wisp of silver cloud hanging above the town. Both of us were alone, one of each of us, everyone else having gone to bed, but for a few stars.

The next day I went to the dining hall for lunch and then afterward to the mailroom, walking slowly, letting the heels of my cowboy boots scrape along. I heard a scraping noise behind me. I glanced over my shoulder. She was walking up the path with Bobbi, scraping the ground with the souls of her shoes, hunched over, head down, moving slowly, hands deep in her pockets, as if imitating a depressed person.

They came up past me in a hurry. "Going to Casino?" I asked them, perking up suddenly in a Cockney accent like Marty Feldman. She walked with her friend, not answering. She turned to her friend, a shorter pretty redhead, asking her in a confiding way leaning close to her.

"Are you going?" she asked the redhead, aloofly, as if Casino were something disagreeable. "Are you," the redhead asked her. Then her answer was muffled, gone in the distance they had put between us and the thickness of coats.

Casino Night, I took my time getting ready. I putzed around in my room. I didn't really feel like going for a while, but then I got dressed. I kept my glasses on.

The room was crowded, steam on the windows, warm, almost prickly. Everyone had arrived already, packing into the room, and my appearance, at eleven must have been one of the last. I had a glass of champagne. Tables covered by white table clothes had been set up about the room offering various games of chance. Klein, the guru of Diplomacy, was dealing black jack, surrounded by his fans. Gurnsey, the popular philosophy professor, who attended toga parties, held court over the crowd gathered, eager to laugh, at the plastic roulette wheel table. Girls sat around at gaming tables and bingo, their dates charmed.

There was a large vertical wheel with numbers on it to be called. I came past a table with a woman student wearing a tight sequined outfit. I kept my eyes up to her face, and so she caught my attention.

"Don't you want to play?" she asked. "It's for a good cause."

"No. Got a gambling problem. Runs in the family."

She looked at me. "Nothing ventured, nothing gained."

"I suppose." I didn't feel like stopping and talking to anyone. That always seems to interfere with my natural thoughts. I hurt all over anyway, and nothing could really change that, except for one thing.

I stood quietly at the back of the room surveying the crowd. I saw her across on the other side of the room, standing in between tables. She was wearing a plain white blouse. She had a glass of champagne in her hand.

She was with a long-faced long-nosed boy I'd seen her with before.

Hersh came up to me.

"Hey, Jamie, I'm sorry I missed your birthday."

"You didn't miss much. I went to see *Blue Velvet* by myself. Fell asleep in the movie theater." I raised my glass. "Cheers." I was a bit ashamed about spending my birthday alone. It had been a shitty night, the worst kind of freezing rain, pouring sleet. I'd seen her in the dining hall at a big round table. I was thinking about saying something to her, but then Bill

Richards corralled me, and then I got a ride back up the hill, and all alone in my room on my birthday in January wasn't any fun either.

Hersh looked around. "So is 'the Queen' here?" That's what they had called her at her school in the City. Hersh had explained that to me. I didn't know who it said more about. I couldn't imagine anyone really calling her that but as a protest against her crown. But maybe she had an imperious way of making you feel like you were the one doing something wrong, never herself.

"Yeah."

"I brought a cigar," he said, surveying the outer edge of turning events. "She's with that guy again," said Hersh, looking across the room, rolling his eyes.

"What do you know about him?"

"He gives rim jobs."

She lofted a cork back over her shoulder into the crowd, putting her arm down quickly, facing forward. She laughed gaily.

Her two friends came toward me on their circuit of the room. I reached out for the balloon strings attached to the back of a nearby chair, pulling the balloons toward me just as they came by. I let the balloons go and they passed me. They stood nearby and then they moved on.

The night went on, and I drank champagne, a bit thirsty but relaxed, perfectly under control on my side of the room, but for the occasional pang of loneliness when I saw a couple.

Then the lights came up. I walked back to the hall to get my coat. Two big guys stood drinking vodka straight from the bottle by the coats. "Here," the close one said, "take a swig."

"Thanks, man," I said, handing the bottle on to the second one, a heavy kid with a crew cut, wiping my lips with the side of my hand.

She and the boy came by and she sat at the edge of the table just across the hallway, the kid standing. He sat down next to her, hunched forward, silent, then saying something. She looked forward as the kid spoke to her. The football players handed me the bottle again so I took another swig. She sat, swinging her feet back and forth, listening for some particular note.

I stood outside of the dining hall watching from a distance as the kid walked her down the sidewalk.

The bulletin board hung next to the open door. I stepped back from the wall as I looked at the listings. H. Kermit Strong had served as Acting President my freshman year. He'd been here as long as anyone.

"Hello," the old man said, turning, his eyebrows raised, his cheeks ruddy. "What's going on?" he said, a twinkle of a wink in his eye, a gentle grin.

"Oh, just out wandering, I guess." I shrugged my shoulders and looked down and couldn't help smiling.

"Hmmm," he said. He moved one piece of paper over onto a neat stack, the next one before him. "Wandering. That's good," he said, distracted for a moment, waiting for a beat of energy to come through the

Universe as it would. "Good way to enter into the dream of the novel.
Essential part of reading, to keep free from distractions." He found what he
was looking for apparently, and raised a sheet of paper closer to his eyes.
"What else can you do? We read all these books, but we don't learn much
about the people who write them."

"No, not much I guess," I said, my hands in my pockets, agreeing.

He looked down over the desk, arms propped on his knuckles, his
silver hair combed back over his head, dark on the sides, his brows dark.

There were two wooden armchairs before the desk. He turned toward
one, and we both sat down.

"Some people who graduate here become writers, of different sorts.
Some work for ad agencies, some for television. You have to pay your bills."
He folded his hand together, tightening his brow. "I kept in touch with one
fellow who was writing dialogue for stag films," he said, leaning forward.
"But that would ruin you."

"Yeah," I nodded. "I bet it's hard to get by in New York."

The old man leaned forward again, bringing his hand to the cuff of his
turtleneck. Out in the darkness, the wind caught a clump of snow hanging on
a branch somewhere above, the crystals dissolving away in the light of the
window.

"Tolstoy wanted to do himself in before he discovered what he
wanted out of life. For a while he was afraid to go out of the house with a
shotgun. Dante climbs out of the dark forest back into the light. These guys
had to write. They had to go through a feeling of futility." He leaned back in
his chair and put his hands behind his head, stretching his back. "Think of

Odysseus. Twenty years of war, adventure, temptations, the bizarre, hostile world one travels in. Protecting your artistic self when there's no immediate pay-off, that's the bravest thing there is. Bravest thing you can do."

"But having to write, that's like admitting you're some sort of cripple, isn't it?"

"No. It's simply seizing a form of expression that one naturally gravitates to. It might feel like a losing battle, maybe, but you have to fight it. Got no choice. That's how it is. There's no other way to do it." He looked at me.

I nodded to him.

"You just have to be working on something. Then it will figure itself out." He leaned back in his chair. "So don't ever let 'em mess with your swing." He leaned forward and I took it to be time to go.

I saw myself out and went up the hall and up the narrow stone steps to the first floor, past the shadowed doorframes toward the exit light.

I walked out into the cold, down the hill, across the road. The air was thin, extending to the stars, the same empty stuff and nighttime. I crossed the old footbridge over the railroad tracks. I walked up the sandy road through the woods, ruts in the icy pine needles, to the observatory, leaving the lights of the street behind. The trees closed in on me pitch black, and then I was at the edge of the clearing. I edged forward into the darkness, the bulk of the observatory glowering before me. I walked across the open field, the pasture grass bent down by a crust of snow.

I found my way down the pasture and through the hedge at the low end of the field into the classical garden, boxwood hedgerows arranged by pebbled paths. I stepped along the hedge to a bench in the middle of a rectangle, not far from the sleeping mansion. A Grecian statue of a woman stood at the end. I liked to look at her face. I'd look at her and ask her questions and she'd try to tell me something behind her stone expression. She had been covered with a wooden box.

I brushed the stone bench off and sat down. I wanted to bring her down here one night. It would be warm then and we would sit there in the night under the stars far away from campus pretending it was our garden. We'd sit there on the bench together and finally we'd talk. We'd talk and she would see how I wasn't crazy and how I believed in myself, how I believed in time and work.

I sat there on the bench, my hands along the front edge, leaning forward. I closed my eyes.

I didn't know it took bravery. I didn't know what bravery was. I was just doing what I thought was the right thing to do, the thing the books and all the learning called you to do. I was just being myself, what I had always been, who I always was, who I always would be.

Then I was walking toward the path down through the hedge to the road. I looked back, the vapor of the house lifting away in the cold from a side pipe. I made it through the gap in the hedge to the sidewalk. I stood underneath the row of old beech trees. The road lay bare, frozen, particles of ice twirling in tiny currents along the surface. And maybe some of us are just meant to be like that, swirling along, over a road somewhere that doesn't mean anything, just loneliness in the night.

The sun got a little stronger, the days a bit longer. I needed Carlson, my advisor, to sign off on my choices for classes my final semester. It came down to the last day to turn the form in to the Registrar's Office. Carlson had his office hours on Fridays from one to two. I walked up to the Chapel at one thirty, the form tucked in under my belt. I came to the door just as he had come out of the Chapel, a tall fine blond woman like a sailing ship following in his wake. He did not look at me as he passed.

"Mr. Carlson, I wondered if you could look this over for me," I said, standing there.

Carlson stopped and turned toward me. I reached under my sweater and pulled out the form, holding it out for him. He took the form, a large index card, into his hand and gave it a quick look through his reading glasses. He didn't say anything.

"Here's a pen," I said.

The woman froze. I looked up to her face again, to find her eyes, and she looked straight at me. I looked down at my sleeve. A thread was coming undone and I tucked it in underneath with my palm. She stood perfectly still, except for a slight turn of her head, as her eyes kept focus on me.

Carlson glanced through the form.

"Thanks," I said.

The woman looked down, her cheekbone touched by a strand of hair that she brushed away with a light smile. She cast her eyes down, and they walked off down the hill together, resuming their quiet conversation. He leaned in toward her slightly, saying something.

I put the form back under my sweater, and turned without looking back, stepping up to the door and entering the hallway. I walked up to the bathroom with the old fixtures, a quiet place with a smoked window. I washed my hands and stood in front of the mirror looking at my face staring back at me.

Then I was ready. I walked down to the Registrar's Office in the old library. There was a line. I came closer to the desk. Then the woman at the computer took my form. She looked down at the green screen and clicked a few things on the keypad. "Okay," she said, smiling quickly up at me.

I turned. The Princess stood in line about ten people behind. As I went past her in the narrow passage I moved my elbow out the slightest inch, brushing her arm. She was looking down too, just as I was, wearing her overcoat, just like I was. Her arm met the touch of mine, an elbow gently against her upper arm, just for a moment as I passed.

CHAPTER EIGHT

The Princess entered the dining hall just as I was about to leave after lunch. I was putting my dad's old cashmere overcoat on, careful of one of the sleeve linings. She came past the television room and turned to the cafeteria line. She unbuttoned the new red overcoat she had since Christmas break. Tossing her hair back, she slipped her arms from her coat, about to place it on a hook. The rack with a row of hooks stood between us.

My arms still stuck out straight, I went stiff all over, hands out straight, fingers parted. I watched her and my legs became stiff like the rest of me, heavy and unbending. I moved forward, my feet coming down with the massive crashing sounds I made with puffed cheeks.

I moved slowly toward her. My monstrous eyes stared straight. She stood where she was, hanging her coat up on the right hook, eyes forward. She tossed her head back, straightening her hair flat behind her.

I moved forward, stiff, slow and menacing. "RRRRGH," I roared softly from deep down in my throat. I flailed my stiff cement arms around clumsily. She stood there.

She didn't moved. I had my arms out straight, webbed iron hands at the ready, the final space between us.

The monster stopped in his tracks. He pondered his monster direction. Monster thoughts went through his mind. The monster looked around with his beady eyes for a moment, pondering his situation. The monster roared tentatively at her.

"Are you a monster?" she asked, without raising her voice.

I roared quietly one more time, in the affirmative. I lowered my arms. The monster stood deflated in his tracks. "Urrrr," he released, looking down at the ground.

Then I was standing there mutely before her, a big sad idiot. "Um, yeah," I said softly.

She turned, narrowing her eyes, moving on now, tossing her head back slightly with a hint of a smile. She stepped forward slowly, pushing off.

I moved away into the foyer. Kareem jumped up from the couch in the television lounge.

"Hey, Warren Beatty, we're having a party tonight."

"Oh, okay."

"You're going to come, right?"

"Sure. Later on."

"Good."

Around midnight I came up to the dormitory building down by the railroad tracks, pulling the glass door open. It was her building. The party was up on her floor. I did not expect her to be there, even if the party was across the hall. She might as well be out of town. I could hear the party above me. Sophomores, having a beer party, music being played in one of the four social rooms, the door kept open. I came up to the top of the stairs.

I heard the small titter of a small crowd. A few heads turned with merry faces, Kareem, the host, a groomed smile, his slick black hair combed back. He came forward. "Hello, my friend." I shook his hand. "I'm glad you could make it."

"Thanks." I looked around for a cup.

"Are you drunk?"

"Not quite."

"We're out of beer."

I looked at him. I looked over at the keg in the trashcan.

A skinny kid came up to us, on the verge of jumping up and down.

"The keg is kicked," the kid shouted in a high voice, twirling around. "The keg is kicked! No more beer." His eyes looked off over my shoulder.

"No more beer! The fucking keg is kicked," he sang, beginning to jump up and down. "Don't you understand?" he yelled, leaning his head back.

"No one talks to a senior that way," I said.

The music from the portable boom box stereo stopped. I stepped forward and the crowd parted. I walked out and down the steps. I was halfway down the first flight when I heard them singing above.

"Jessica Dorfmann's boyfriend, Jessica Dorfmann's boyfriend..."

More voices joined in unison, laughing out loud.

"Jessica Dorfmann's boyfriend," they sang, louder now, leaning out over the balcony. "Jessica Dorfmann's boyfriend."

I went down the stairs without looking back, across the next landing, down each step to the bottom. I pushed the door open, one of those glass ones in a stainless steel frame with a light steel bar across it, the kind you find on store fronts.

I stepped out into the cold and walked away.

I had tried to call her several times from the library on three separate afternoons roughly the same time. Each time the Princess's roommate Laura answered, and each time I got the same story, no, she was not there. Okay, thanks, thanks a lot. I didn't think she'd be at the party.

I watched the band set up.

"Let's go have a glass of scotch," Martinez said.

"Okay," I said. I didn't really feel like drinking, but what the hell, I followed Martinez up the grand staircase. He had a room up on the second floor at the front of the house.

"Here," Martinez said, handing me a short neat glass of good scotch. Martinez leaned back. We were drinking from the crystal tumblers his old man the doctor had given him. His eyes darted around, checking on the pile of books.

"So how's your thesis going?"

"It's going pretty good. It's a lot of work. Pshoo." He told me I looked like Joyce again. The thesis was something he wanted to do. He wanted to write plays. He had been pre-med the first two years.

We went downstairs and stood by the mantle of the fireplace in the ballroom of the house. The band was playing, getting warmed up.

I saw the Princess come in the room with her girlfriend, the Greek one. They came and stood at the other end of the mantle. I didn't even look at her. I picked up my glass and took a sip.

"Would you like another? Let's go back upstairs," Martinez said.

"No, I'm fine." I looked at the band playing. "I'll probably just go get a beer."

I handed the glass back to Martinez.

"I'm going to go do a little bit more work," Martinez said, and went back upstairs.

I went down to the basement where the tap was. I walked back through the plywood-paneled hallway to the stairs the beer in my hand, taking a sip off it so it wouldn't spill. I went and stood against the wall of the front hallway, the double doors to the ballroom to my right, the front door and windows opposite.

Vincent came in the front door and saw me standing there. He stood against the wall next to me.

"I'm going to go get a beer. You want one?"

"Nah, no thanks. I got one."

He came back later and stood along the wall with me. I didn't have much to say.

He leaned against me and I put my arm over his shoulder.

"Are you doing alright?" he asked.

"Yeah, I'm fine." I watched them come and go. I could hear the music fine. I felt far away.

Two young girls came out of the ballroom. I guessed they came from Smith. One, a short girl, with bobbed hair, looked over at us standing there. She leaned over to her friend.

"Oh my god, look at those two gay guys over there hugging each other," the one said, trying to be quiet.

I laughed out loud and smiled, looking at them. The one was embarrassed and walked past us. The girl looked very young. She had not expected to be noticed. I watched them walk quickly away. I thought about going to catch them and take them out dancing, but I didn't feel like it.

The Princess came out and stood with her girlfriend near the front door. The kid she was with at Casino Night had just come in. He took his coat off, throwing it over the top of a chair. Then they were all laughing over some introductory joke and the kid was enjoying her company. It was nice to watch, after all.

I could not miss seeing them. I saw how gay she was, how charmed the kid was. She was drinking something from a cup, bringing it up to her lips, smiling over it. She appeared quite happy, talkative, smiling broadly, convivially laughing. I warmed up to it. I couldn't hear what they were talking about, but I saw the kid's delight now that he was accepted into her presence in public. I looked away.

The band was playing well, moving on to familiar songs. She walked by with her entourage through the double doors of the ballroom. "Fine with me," I thought as she walked past, showing herself in profile, as if she were watching me out of the very corners of her eyes. I felt there was some sort of interest with which she watched me.

The kid had passed by me. All he knew was that he was going to the dance floor with her.

Bill Richards arrived. He had been studying. "Come on, Jamie," he said in imitation of a geology professor, "let's go examine the dance floor."

We crossed through the double doors into the ballroom, the music louder. The band was playing mellower music now, a decent rendition of the Modern English song that everyone liked to sing along with.

"*I'll stop the world and melt with you*," the crowd half-shouted atonally, along with the band. Then the band did the quiet part. I was standing toward the back.

Then the band went into an Elvis Costello.

"*Allison, my aim is... true*," the crowd sang along with the guitar player. I thought how it was nice music to dance to if you had a girl.

I heard something indistinctly from somewhere on the dance floor, half-noticing it.

"Hey," I felt Bill poking me. "Did you see that?"

"No, what'd I miss?" I said, leaning forward to hear Bill, so I could hear him.

"She was dancing with that skinny kid and then all of a sudden she's gone."

I looked around. She was gone. The kid was gone.

I listened to the band for a little while longer. Then I left the dance floor and walked back out into the hall. The Princess was nowhere to be seen.

I walked past the front door. It was a cold night out. I went downstairs for another beer. I was drinking through the top foam—the kid at the tap was a bit rude, I thought--when I saw the kid pacing around in the corner of the basement. He was frantic about something, going over some sort of conversation, wringing his hands, throwing them up in the air, pulling at his hair almost.

I had never been like that. I walked away, leaving the kid down in the basement.

I walked up the steps and stood by the door, just inside the ballroom, sipping my beer contentedly. It tasted good. The band had stopped, and the lights had come up.

The kid was paying for it now. The kid was down in the basement still, blaming himself. Maybe she did that to a lot of people, being a princess and all.

I wondered why I hadn't had another beer earlier. I saw the Greek girlfriend of hers looking at me. She stood her ground.

I went downstairs for another beer and the kid was still there, pacing.

The next day I went and sat in the library after brunch. I was looking out the window, an open notebook in front of me, when Peter came by.

"What are you doing, Beastie?"

"Not much."

"I'm going to take out *Phantom of the Opera*. You want to watch it?"

"Lon Chaney?"

"Yeah, the original."

"When are you going to watch it?"

"In about an hour or so."

"Maybe. I'd like to."

"Okay. If you want to just come by later."

"I'm going to write for awhile, I think."

Peter looked at me for a moment.

"Yeah, I'm going to try to get some work done."

"Alright. I'll catch you later."

"I'll be done before dinner."

"Good."

Peter walked back to the doors leading out to the mezzanine above the lobby, carpeted orange.

I sat there awhile, looking down from time to time at the blank page before me. "The original," I said to myself.

I gathered my papers and walked out to the mezzanine, then down the stairs, past the reading room with the lounge chairs out through the magnetic detector by the front desk and out the doors, down the steps. The quad lay before me.

I went into town to find her Valentine card at the store where I had found the birthday card for my father. I found this Gary Larson card with a warthog in the picture, warthogs at a party. Two lady warthogs are seated at a table, a guy warthog in a Hawaiian shirt standing, looking over at them. "Oh, if it isn't God's gift to warthogs," one of the lady warthogs says to the other, rolling her eyes, the guy warthog doing his best to look suave.

I put a line through the greeting, "Happy Birthday, you party animal." I wrote in "Happy Valentine's Day" above the line I crossed out. I addressed it to her college post office box, and dropped it in the mail slot in the mailroom after lunch the next day. She would get it by Valentine's Day.

Valentine's Day came. I went to the mailroom after lunch. I opened my box. There was a card in it. I pulled it out, along with some college announcements. It was from my mother.

That night I sat down with Gould and Rosenstern at dinner. The Princess's friends came and sat down at the next table. Each time I glanced over another seemed to be looking at me.

I called her later in the week.

Friday night after dinner I walked down the hill to her dorm, opening the glass door and walking up to the third floor. I knocked on the outer door to the main room, but no one answered so I opened the door and walked in across the room. Steps lead down to a landing, four rooms off the landing, two on each side, the bathroom straight ahead.

"Hello-oh," I said, knocking on her door, and after a moment and some indistinguishable noises she came, opening the door. She looked up at me. She came out, slipping past him into the bathroom, not saying anything. "Hi," I said, after her.

She went to the sink and raised some water to her face. I turned the water on in the other sink, the one closest to the door, and bent down with my head at the tap to take a quick drink of water. She was not saying anything, and ducked toward the stall, then came around me back toward her room. I let her go forward and then I followed after her. She was flushed.

"I'm sorry, were you taking a nap?"

She stood facing me in the doorway of her room, the door close to her, so that I could not see into the room.

"I was just seeing what you were up to tonight. Nothing, yet, I guess."

"Why do you come here?" she said, awake now. "We never go out on dates or anything. We never go to movies together or to dinner," she said calmly, tossing her head back slightly and looking back.

She held the door. She pulled the door closer to her.

"Well that's 'cause you'd say no."

"Well, yeah," she said, quickly. "Of course. You keep at it anyway."

"Just 'cause you analyzed me once," I said.

She was about to say something.

"There's nothing about me you wouldn't like," I said. I stepped back off a foot, seeing now the full-length mirror off to the side by the steps to the common room.

Something quieted her, and she stood in the doorway, letting it open just a little more, slightly. She looked into my eyes, remembering something.

She raised a scoffing sound as she let what I said register.

"Except personal," I said looking at her.

She stood there, looking down for a moment, relaxed, if she could have been.

"Well, have a good night," I said. I climbed the stairs, crossed the social room without looking back, opened the door and left.

I walked into town, bought a six pack of cheap can beer at *Russell's* on Main Street and went back up to the house. It was too early for the parties to start. No one was around except Rich, the resident counselor, sitting in front of the television.

I sat down on the couch next to him and cracked open a beer.

"I went by this girl's dorm room tonight. You know her, the one from Valentine Hall last year I was telling you about."

"Jessica..."

"Dorfmann, yeah. Well, anyway, I went up there."

"What happened?"

"'We never go out,' she says, like 'get it through your thick head that I don't like you one bit.' Christ."

The counselor was friendly, but not any good for anything. He looked at me through his round wire-framed glasses, distant from such problems.

"We had a stream running behind my house. The clearest water. It came down through our woods, from the hills above. We'd listen to it through the open windows in the summer when we went to sleep. There was a swamp my brother and I played in. You couldn't swim in it, but it was nice. Frogs croaking."

"You okay?"

"Fine."

I went down to the party at Chi Phi and planted myself at the end of the bar down in the basement drinking beer. When I got up to pee a stocky woman with short hair, a fine arts major, stood before me in the hallway. "You're the talk of the party," she said, smiling at me.

"Oh. How so?" I mumbled.

"All these girls downstairs were talking about you."

"What?" I said.

"I don't know, some sophomore girls, I think. Down in the hallway."

I looked away. "What sort of things?"

"They were saying, 'Aww, Jamie,' and things like that."

"They must have been joking... making fun of me or something."

"No, I don't think so."

I saw two of them, but they didn't look over at me so I went through the dark hallway to the narrow stairway back up to the dance floor. But then I thought how another of them seemed to look at me out of the darkness as I went up the hallway from the taproom to find the staircase leading up to the central entrance hall of the house. I had missed the look in the darkness, moving forward, but now it partly registered, even though I could only ignore it and just go my own way.

That week I was coming out of the dining hall. I had my arms in my overcoat, straightening it over my shoulders.

"How are you doing?" the fine arts major with the short hair and a face staring at something beyond you said.

"Oh I'm fine, thanks," I said, trying to smile, coming up with one, nodding to her. I didn't feel like talking. Behind me I heard a different female voice say, "no, you're not."

I turned around behind me as I pushed the door open. A tall young woman, a junior, stood at the desk where they checked your ID so that you could go in and eat. She was looking down at the students raising money for their humor newspaper. She could not help smiling at her own cleverness.

She looked away still, as if to offer me something impersonally. I looked back at her for a moment.

I walked away down the ramp, hatless into the cold, the brightness on the melted-down snow of the open yard before the hall.

The next weekend I went to a party down at TD. Barbara Dean stood alone against a wall by the dance floor. She looked a gypsy. I liked the coldness of the look on her face, the absence of expression as she looked back at me, under no illusion. I had a few beers already. We talked for a little while above the music, and then she did not move away. We went downstairs. I had another beer. She lit a cigarette.

"Do you want to go dance?"

"Sure." She took a puff and put out the cigarette.

We had not danced long when she said it was getting late. "Would you walk me home?"

We went the back way up the quiet street. "I have to pee." I went to pee by the last house, in the yard, behind some trees. A light went on above the side door of the house, and then a pot-bellied bearded man opened the screen door and peered out from the side porch.

"Could you could please be quiet." We had been giggling about something, and the connection had already been made and there was nothing to get in its way now.

"I'm sorry."

"And please go to the bathroom somewhere else."

"Yes, I will. Sorry."

I gathered myself up.

We walked away taking a right and coming around the low quiet garage. "Sorry about that. I was afraid he was going to call the cops when the light went on, but he was cool about it."

We came to her house. She lived up on the third floor of the Chi Psi house. "You're a few doors down from Vincent."

"Yes, he lives right there."

"Nice view from his room. I was checking it out."

We came to her door and she opened it without any questions.

"Would you like a glass of wine?"

"Sounds great."

She went behind a batik curtain and came back with a glass of red wine. "Fancy. Thanks a lot."

There was one light on in the room, underneath a tie-dyed bandanna. She lit three candles.

"Do you like *Roxy Music*?"

"I love *Roxy Music*."

She went to a stereo and put in a CD. The first notes came into the dimly lit room flickering with candlelight. She was sitting on the futon.

"Avalon," I said.

"Yes. Come over here."

Then we did not waste any time. And then it was over too soon and I was very tired and I slept.

It was light when I woke, a feeling of electric fuzziness in my head. I reached for my pants. She sat up in bed, pulling the covers up over her high breasts.

"God, I feel like hell," I said, pulling my pants up.

"There's some juice in the fridge."

"That would be good."

She put a tee shirt on, got up and reached for the small refrigerator, pouring orange juice in a plastic beer cup.

"Thanks."

I drank the juice, sitting down in the chair by her desk. I put my shoes on. I stood and turned toward the window.

"Let me check out your view."

She sat silently, leaning back against the wall behind her bed, her arm draped over toward her side of the bed.

"Well, I gotta go. Probably back to bed."

"Get some Gatorade."

"Good idea. How do you feel?"

"Not so bad.

"Well," I said, finding my coat by the door. "It was nice hanging out with you," I said at the door, then opening it.

She looked back, though I didn't really look at her. I did not know what to give her.

No one was in the hall.

It was a sunny day, and I squinted, coming out the side door, looking at my watch to see if I could catch brunch at the dining hall. It was too early.

I walked down to the Common and across it to the sidewalk, past the Presbyterian church with the grand old Cadsura tree--my father explained how it had been one of the first in America, brought over as a seedling from Japan--around the town hall and up the hill. It was already there, the guilt.

I went to dining hall at noon. I came out of the line. Bob, Spike, Peter and Stanley were sitting around.

"Hey, Beastie."

"Hey, guys."

"What'd you do last night?"

"Slept with Barbara Dean," I said lowly.

"Arright! Good for you man."

"Eh," I said shrugging off the pat on the back.

"Why, eh?" said Stanley.

"I just don't feel so good about it."

"Why not? Got some ginchie-ginchie."

"I don't know. No, I'm not sorry. Just that..."

"Don't worry about it. It's good for you."

"I guess so."

I looked down at the burger now that I had dressed it and put the bun back on. I picked up a French fry, eating it. I touched my napkin with my fingertips.

"Maybe it's just that I feel like hell. Red wine."

"Oh, you were drinking wine?"

"Well, of course I was pretty drunk. Had a whiskey at happy hour, then beer. Then wine up in her room. Never mixes."

They all looked at me. I put my hand on my soda glass.

"Bestial One. Beastie Boy."

"I just get so goddamn lonely, not having a girl. Then I finally can't take it any longer and I pounce."

They all laughed at the image.

I looked down at my plate before me and took a tentative bite from the cheeseburger, chewing it carefully before swallowing it. I took a sip of Coke and then I knew I could burp and that it wouldn't all come back up again.

There were warm days, and then it was cool again. The phone on the wall outside my door rang.

"Hello?"

"Hey. What's going on?"

"Oh, not much, I guess."

"I need you to do me a favor."

"Sure."

"I need you to go buy some flowers."

"Okay."

"And then if you could bring them up to Deb up at Mount Holyoke for me."

"Sure."

"Good. Do you have fifty bucks lying around?"

"Yeah," I said, somewhat proudly, though it wasn't much.

"I'll send you a check for fifty bucks."

"What kind of flowers should I get?"

"Just go down to the florists and tell him, I don't know, a Spring Mix or something and tell him how much you're spending."

"Just tell him fifty bucks worth."

"Yeah, basically. Call him up, and then the next day he'll have them ready for you."

"Okay, so you want me to do this when?"

"How about... Saturday, in the afternoon."

"All right. Yeah, I can just take the bus up."

"Right. And she lives in Canter Hall. You'll have to ring at the front desk."

"The front desk."

"Yes, you go there and she'll come down."

"What if she's not there?"

"She'll be there. And if not, you can just leave them and they'll get to her."

"Okay."

"Cool. Thanks a lot."

"No problem."

"So how are things going?"

"Ahhh. All right I guess."

"You been getting laid at all?"

"No."

"Maybe some chick up at Holyoke will see you carrying flowers..."

"And take pity on me."

"It'll make them think you got a girlfriend..."

"Yeah."

"Which makes you all the more attractive to them," my brother said, slowly.

"Ah," I said. "I see how it's played." I knew that already.

The next afternoon I walked down into town to the florists. The clerk reached into the cooler for the bundle. The flowers were wrapped in light paper shaped like a flattened cone. It was a good-sized package, light to carry. I walked back with the bundle of flowers and sat on the steps in front of the old library waiting for the campus bus that went by Hampshire and then up the hill to Mount Holyoke. I felt proud of myself. The bus came. I looked out the windows as the bus drove south, stopping at Hampshire College, then up the hill.

Deb came running to the door, as if she had been waiting for me. She looked at the flowers. She was with one of her girlfriends. "These are from your man in Boston," I said, delivering my line.

"Oh thank you."

"My pleasure." I stood there for a moment.

"Thanks again," Deb said quickly with a prepared smile. "Bye."

I waited for the bus, watching a few of the Holyoke girls walk up the street, one of them very pretty by the looks of her as she walked away. The bus came--it was sunnier out now--and I got on the bus and the bus rolled away along the bare trees lining the avenue, making a throaty sound underneath the seats. The fairways of the golf course, surprising patches of green, lay separated by stands of pine and fingers of shrunken snow.

Now the bus pulled up the long hill that the college sat up on, taking the right to pull up before the old library. I walked down to the corner in an aimless mood. I was near the stop sign when I saw her coming toward me on the sidewalk across the street. She was walking back from town in her thoughtful way, her ankle rolling her right foot out. Then I knew it was her, seeing the long legs, the way they came into her hips, the demure prettiness of her face even at a distance. I moved so that the stop sign fell in the direct line between us.

There was something about seeing her calves, her feet in light thin shoes like slippers, that made me think of home somewhere, somewhere close, or maybe far off, like a distant light in the sky as it clears after a thunderstorm at dusk in the fall, right as darkness moves in. Her legs made me feel soft and calm, warm inside.

The Princess stopped at the opposite corner and looked before crossing the crosswalk. She checked up the street for traffic coming from Northampton. Then she was gliding across the street and then on the sidewalk. She turned to walk down along the road in the direction of the dining hall. I fell in beside her, walking on the muddy grass between the sidewalk and the snow piles.

"Hey, Pal," I said gently in a high bird-like voice, cracked slightly in the way a voice is that hasn't said anything in some time. I was relaxed. Whatever.

I had to look down to avoid the muddier spots.

There was a second or two before she responded, biding her time for the moment. There was a white paper bag in her hand. She was just on the verge of smiling. Her head was tilted to the side away from him, as if she were considering whether or not to taste something placed before her.

"Why don't you walk on the sidewalk. You'll ruin your shoes."

"Oh, thanks." I looked down at my loafers.

I moved on to the sidewalk proudly beside her. Her smile broadened just slightly.

"How are your classes?"

"They're fine."

She allowed another smile, looking ahead.

"What are you taking?"

"An English class, a sociology class, history and an art history."

"What English class?"

"An English class," she said loftily. "They're all the same."

"Oh," I said, grinning.

"How are your roommates?" I said, taking a breath in.

"Oh, they're fine." Another sort of expression came to her face. "They're territorial sometimes," she said quietly.

"I guess."

"Laura is sick. I went into town to get her something."

"Some medicine?"

"No, just something to make her feel better."

"Well, that's very nice of you to take care of your roommates," I said. "Does she have the flu?"

"Just a head cold."

"Oh, I'm sorry," I said. "Yeah. That's going around."

We walked along a bit. The sun was out in full now.

"How are your parents?" I asked.

"They're fine. They went skiing for the first time, up in Vermont."

"Hot dog! That's awesome."

I walked in step with her, looking over at her. She looked about, the pine boughs swaying lightly in the gentle breeze, at the slope of the land below the art museum.

She bit her lip. I caught a glance at her long golden hair, so close, seeing it's complexity in the light. I looked down at the silver slippers on her feet.

"I like your slippers," I said.

"Are you daring to make fun of my silver slippers," she said, her voice rising in a chiding way.

"No, they're kind of special."

We were getting closer to her dorm. She reached into the paper pharmacy bag and pulled out a white stuffed rabbit, clean, plump and immaculate.

"Awwww," I said, looking down at it, at the way she held it happily. "Wittle Bunny Wabbit," I said happily, seeing her holding it.

She held the stuffed animal like a baby, smiling in her own radiant way. We were at the door now. I stopped. She stopped and turned to me.

"Are you gonna go see *Jungle Book*?" I asked, looking down, imitating Bashful. The movie was playing that weekend on campus.

"Walt Disney?" she said, incredulously.

"Well, I'm gonna go see it," I said.

I watched her open the door. She didn't say anything. There was a curious expression on her face.

She turned toward the door and then looked back at me. I stood there for a moment, watching her go up to the landing.

I felt so good I went to the library and read from a Hemingway biography, filled with the notion of the great positive force Hemingway's writing had brought to humanity. I made jottings and mental notes about my project, feeling I had made great progress. I was deep into it when Gould came up to my table. We walked down to the dining hall.

I saw her coming up the hill with two of her girlfriends. I felt reassured by our walk together. I let them pass and go on ahead into the dining hall.

I ate dinner with Gould and lingered around long enough in the foyer 'til she came back with two of her roommates. The sick one, the watchdog, was not joining them tonight. She walked slowly out of the hall down the ramp. I watched her red-coated figure depart into the darkness. I did not worry about it, the chemistry of elation still flowing.

The next day a heavy sleet fell over the entire valley, the sound rustling everywhere, from the ground upward, from the heights of black oaks. It fell on my bare head as I walked down from the hill for brunch. I went to the line at the middle dining hall, West.

The Princess was working behind the line serving scrambled eggs from a stainless bin with a big spoon. I came down the line, sliding my tray along. She turned away as I came in front of her. She stepped away from the line toward the big sink and the radio on the shelf, where a student was washing a large pot. She stood there with her back turned, not doing anything. The full-time woman took up the egg-serving spoon.

I took my plate and put it back down on my tray. I went out and sat down with Vincent. He had taken my picture for the yearbook.

"*The Tears* are playing down at UMass tonight," he said.

"They've got that song about the rain, right?" I said, testing the potatoes with my fork.

"It'll be good. It's a Sunday. What's there to do on Sunday?"

"Maybe."

"Oh, come on."

I ate my eggs. The movie was playing one final night.

"I'm going to go get a banana," I said.

I walked toward the second door of the room where the food was served. I could hear the radio behind the line near the back shelves playing the opening riff of *My Girl*. I picked a coffee cup up from the rack. I went to the fruit bowl and found a suitable banana. She was back at the serving line. I started to open my mouth to say hi to her. She had already turned away.

I stood there for a moment. I felt people turn toward me. She glanced at the wall behind me, her chin raised, staring past me. I stood, looking for something to hold onto, some prop to grab, the melodic voices rising in harmony, "*my girl, my girl, my girl, talkin' 'bout, my gir-irl...*"

I walked out into the hall again, and sat back down at the table, agreeing to go to the concert that night.

Leaving, I took my coat from the hook of the rack, putting it on automatically, and stepping out through the heavy door out on to the sidewalk along the Belchertown Road. The wet sleet had picked up, humming with a steady throb beyond the cold edges of the door, driving down on the ice-covered ground. I stepped down to the crosswalk and stopped. I stood there, bareheaded, the top of my head getting soaked, letting it all come down on me. The sleet fell on my face, on my shoulders, soaking my heavy overcoat. I stood there, frozen. I heard a car pass by, seeing its tires, its form slipping along beyond the curb.

I turned to glance back at the windows. I could not see past the reflections with the angle of the gray light. Melted droplets dripped down from my brow.

That night after dinner I stood in the TV lounge, smoking a cigarette. Vincent came up to me.

"Come on, let's go to the concert."

I saw her as she walked by. She lingered at a distance, and I stood there smoking the cigarette, turned away from her.

"Yeah, okay," I said.

We drove down through the rain to the University in a small *Toyota*.

The concert hall was a dark unfinished concrete room. Few, in fact, had turned out. The band went through their set, obligatorily, looking forward, dulled by life on the road away from England. My ears rang with echoed blurs by the end of the first songs. Finally they played their pop hit. The lead singer pissed his pants.

Monday night I went into the library. The new issue of *National Geographic* would be out in the magazine room in the front of the library to the right behind glass doors and past the low lounge reading chairs. The Princess was sitting there with a book on her lap. Two of her girlfriends sat with her. Right before her chair there was a padded stool. I sat down on it before her. "What'ch you reading?" I asked quietly.

She stood up without saying anything, holding a thick book in her hands as if she were about to slam it down on the ground.

"You don't have to get up," I said. I stood up. In a single motion I turned away from her, toward the magazine rack. I reached with one hand, deftly removing the new issue of the *National Geographic*, its cover shining, trimmed with a pleasing yellow, from the shelf. I turned away and walked back out past the row of reading chairs that looked out on the quad.

I went back through the glass doors and sat down at the round table just outside them, adjacent to the shelves with the newly published books upon them, the circulation desk and the metal detector by the door across from me on the other side of the orange carpet. I held the magazine in my hands.

Soon afterward her roommate Laura came out. She stood by the glass doors, studying me. I looked at the pictures in an article about wolves.

The *Geographic*'s new issue held hints about what my life was going to be like. I'd grow up one day and be a mountain climber in the Himalayas or traveling along somewhere by truck or by train, somewhere far away, about to discover something. I was done with it after a few minutes. I closed it, putting it down on the round table rather than putting it back on the shelf. I went up the carpeted steps to the second floor.

CHAPTER NINE

I went and sat out in front of the library on the granite base with my back against the wall, my legs out before me. I took my shirt off. I had a Hemingway biography in my hands. It had nothing to do with any schoolwork.

I heard them coming up from the walk leading from the dining hall, their voices carrying through the pines on the far side of the wide steps, the Princess with her close circle of friends. They turned as a group from the sidewalk and came up the steps. They were all going in together. I looked at my book.

I could not make out what they were talking about, but they sounded like Socractic philosophers. "Well, he is funny though," Laura said. It carried so that I could hear it.

"Well, yes," the Princess said. She paused at the door. It looked as if she were listening to something. I sat in the sun with my book.

Later that week, I drove home for Spring Break. Cricket was ill. My dad said over the phone that it was very serious. I made myself a few ham sandwiches in the dining hall to take with me like Lindbergh.

It began snowing around Herkimer, big light flakes in the car's headlights, turning into a squall. I slowed, trusting the car's footing on the highway road, the sensation of forward motion lost against the steady snowfall before the windshield.

It was snowing still as I pulled in off the Thruway at Utica, rolling up to the green light of the tollbooth. The flakes tumbled down peacefully, big and wet, not about to add up. I rounded the village green, passing the fountain in the center ringed with spruce trees, the nymph statue lit from below with her arm stretched upward, the top ends of her covered with white. Beyond the spruces the shop windows of Park Row hung dark beneath the Christmas lights hung in the trees along the sidewalk. The road curved, and I downshifted through the traffic light, slowing past the steeple-less Presbyterian Church and the old apothecary window on the other side of the street. The street was wet, white at the edges, the tracks of the previous car about to be covered. I glanced into the window of the Village Tavern. It was empty. There was an old barbershop next to the tavern and one across the street, both with traditional candy cane barber poles. I drove slowly past the Rok, through the next traffic light, passing the high school. It was quiet, but still, it was good to be back, good to see it all again.

I came in with my brown Beans duffel bag. "You made good time," my dad said.

Cricket, lying on the floor on her side, had not moved. I got down beside her on the shag carpet. There was a slight opening of her eyes, staring vacantly ahead. "Hello, Cricket," I said softly, touching her head very lightly. "Good dog." She moved her tongue slightly. I saw the swelling past her ribcage underneath the wiry red fur of her side.

My father came back out into the living room. "She's having a tough time."

I looked up and nodded. "Yeah."

"Yesterday was the first day she didn't get up at all. I made an appointment for tomorrow."

"Down at Alberding's?"

"Yes."

"Okay."

I sat down on the floor, rubbing the soft fur at the base of her ears. Her brown eyes were watery, open narrowly, and she did not turn them up to look at me but for a brief second. She looked a long way off, at somewhere very far away. A tide was coming in to lift her and take her from where it came.

"Get yourself a beer, Jamie," Dad called from the kitchen, clearing his throat. I could smell rice cooking.

"Okay." I got up and came into the kitchen, reached to open the door of the fridge and took out a beer. I put the beer on the table just outside the open kitchen, came back and took out silverware from the drawer to set the table. We tried to put away from us what would happen tomorrow.

We sat down and ate. "There's this part in Hamlet where Horatio is asked if he's there on the parapet, and he says, 'Aye, a piece of him,'" I said. "I like that. A piece of him." I picked up my fork again.

We had coffee and I put the dishes away. I sat down by the dog. She hadn't moved. Her eyes closed and then opened slightly. She could not see the things that were close in front of her.

Where be your gibes now? Your gambols, your songs, your flashes of merriment that were wont to set the table on a roar?

We woke up to rain. The little dog had gone further away now. Dad went downstairs to the utility closet to get a shovel. I watched him from the window in my room open the back of the car and put in a cardboard box. "I'll get a towel," he said. He came back with a towel and got down to pick up the dog, cradling her as she lay limp. "Come on," he said softly to the dog. We drove out of town on Harding then out past Reservoir Road.

The dogs always knew they were close to home after a long trip, waking up in the back whenever we made the turn-off onto Reservoir, infallibly. We kept going straight on Twelve B.

Maybe it's the last part of going home that is the hardest. The last mile or so. It's easy up 'til then, and then all your thoughts come. You sense home from a mile away. And when you get close, you feel everything, everything that's happened. You feel the magnetic power of home. Maybe you want to slow down as you approach, so you can stop just outside and look in, to see what you would see if it weren't yours. All the beauty of it you feel. Your house, your home, your mom, your dad, your brother.

The dog, riding in the back of the station wagon, feels the overwhelming beauty of the home, rising from its curled slumber, lifting her head, smiling, tongue out, tasting the magnetic swirling airs of home.

"We'll take her up to Ernst Road later," my father said. I looked off across the field. The clouds were low, the woods enveloping the road, a light rain pattering the windshield. We drove into Deansboro, turning left for the valley road to Waterville. We came into the town, at the top of a low wooded hill, and turned up the main street and then we were in front of the vets.

My father moved with a certain quickness now. He opened the side door and lifted the dog up. "Why don't you get the box now and bring that along with us."

"Okay."

The examination room with a stainless table was small and brightly lit. A chemical odor pervaded the entry. It was a good deal simpler than I had expected. The walls were bare. The vet, a short spectacled man who worked with farm animals, was standing by the stainless steel examination table.

"Hello, Gene," the vet nodded. "Well, I guess its time."

"Yes, I think so."

The doctor had the needle ready. My Dad held her. She didn't move or react to the needle in her forepaw. Then she sagged, her head fell to one side, and the doctor nodded that it was over. Her tongue hung out of her mouth. She lay on her side on the steel table. Then my father, reached down, bent over, and picked her up and cradled her in his arms, her head hanging down as he brought her close to his chest. He placed her down on the towel and wrapped it over her gently all the way. He said nothing. I clamped my lips.

In a thick, low and quiet voice my father said, "Well, I'll write you a check." He blew his nose into a handkerchief, stood for a moment, then went over the table and wrote out the check, leaning down over the checkbook as he did, so to see better. Then he blew his nose again and blinked his eyes.

We were outside the vet's in the rain. My dad stood in his blue trench coat with the box in his arms. I opened the back and moved the shovel aside. He put the box in. I looked across the street as my dad got in. I didn't bother trying not to cry. It was okay to cry a lot. Then I got in.

We drove back, taking the turn up Champion. The rain was light, but steady. The wipers went back and forth. The fields were bare.

We got to top of our old property. A lot of little trees the size of your finger were pressing up out of the ground, an old pasture. I pressed the shovel down. The ground was hard. The shovel blade hit rocks with a clank. I had to bend down and grip them lose. "I think that's good," Dad said, after I'd worked on the hole. My father put the box down in the hole, leaning over. "There you go," he said.

We each tossed a handful of dirt on the box, standing there a moment. My father looked down into the hole. I watched him through the water that was in my eyes. It was something you tried to remember, and felt keenly, and yet, in a sort of shock, you can't remember it so clearly.

We drove back down the winding wooded road, past the old house, down through the woods, past the reservoir. It was raining still, the clouds shifting in the low sky above us, as if they were sorting something out.

"Death is a necessary part of life, Jamie," my dad said, looking as he made the turn onto College Street at the blinking light. The windshield wipers moved the pattering droplets of rain away to the sides and a wind took them past. "It would be a cruel fate to go on living forever. It is inevitable that things come to an end." He shrugged and looked forward with his eyes widened briefly then turning his neck slightly.

I nodded and looked back at him.

We drove on.

The next day I drove to Syracuse, taking the thruway rather than the slow Route 5 to save time.

"Hello, hello," my mother said when I stood at the door as she came down the stairs. She opened the door and hugged me.

"Hi, Ma."

"I'm sorry about Cricket. Are you doing all right?"

"Yeah, I'm okay."

"I wish I had been there."

"Well, it would have been nice to invite you."

We were in the kitchen. The cat, Tinkerbell, jumped up on the table and stood looking out the window through the curtain. The man next door ran a garage. It was dark out.

A roasting chicken was in the oven, with onions around it. There was a plate of Triscuits and New York Sharp Cheddar. I took a sip off my wine. It was warm in the kitchen.

"Sweetheart, you have all the talent in the world," my mom said, picking up her wine glass. "If some snobby girl won't give you a tumble, forget about her. There are other fish in the sea, as my aunt Pauline used to say. Once she had Tommy drive her down to B.C. where Erin was in the middle of a blizzard just to tell her that. 'There are other fish in the sea.' Then they turned around and went back."

It was a warm day when I got back to school. It was lunchtime and I saw her at the dining hall. She was leaving with her friends. As they walked out she stopped to peruse the ice cream tubs in the freezer by the open arch out into the hallway. Her highly evolved peripheral vision registered being in my line of sight. She lingered for a moment, and then she turned and left, the ice cream having bored her. I wanted not to do anything, but then I changed my mind. It was as if a chase had been announced. I waited two beats, and rose on cue. I swept up my tray, took it to the dish window and was up the hall not far after her. I grabbed my coat and swung out of the hall and down the wooden ramp just as she was heading down the sidewalk back to her dorm.

"Hello," I said, in a basso tone, beside her now. "How was your break?" I kept to the same musical note.

She said nothing. She was moving ahead quickly.

"Okay. Well, I was glad I went home. We had to put our dog to sleep."

"I don't want to talk to you," she declared, raising her chin.

"Oh, you'll talk to me right now," I said, chiding gently, continuing the opera.

She turned and grabbed the ground with her feet, firmly. "I don't want to talk to you!" she said, slowly and emphatically, in a high note that rose above the orchestra and the chorus.

I found myself facing her, conscious that I was looking at her through my glasses.

"Well," I said. "Fuck." It came out louder than I had intended.

She looked at me, still, awakened, as if she had found something she had been looking for.

I stepped toward her, brushing past her. "Sorry," I said, walking quickly away.

"Yeah, my dog died," I thought, walking up the side street that led to the bottom of the hill.

I took the ball out when I got home and threw it against the brick wall of the house on the side of the long sloping yard for a good long time.

After class and lunch Friday I went down to the Office of Career Counseling to look over the heavy bound computer listings of alumni professions. I went in and took my spot in the low chair next to the listings, looking through the lists for the offbeat occupations, for those who had gone to Montana to be cattle ranchers and things of that sort. I had a vague idea that I might directly contact one of them and ask if I could come out to visit. I liked sitting behind Mrs. Keating's desk with a book reading the listings in my lap.

A thin silver-haired stooped old man wearing a gray suit poked his head in through the open door and walked in. He stood a moment once inside.

"Well, hello," said Mrs. Keating, having retained her British accent. She stood up, beaming. "If it isn't our Mr. Ferral. What a nice surprise."

"Hello, dear," the man said.

"Wonderful," Mrs. Keating said, wagging back and forth.

The Princess appeared gracefully through the open doorway into the room. She stopped a moment, glanced briefly at me, and then turned to the far wall. She stood for a moment holding the strap of her bag over her shoulder, touching the shelf of an array of magazine-like brochures. Then she took her bag down, reached into it for a pen and a notepad, and set the bag down beside her. She picked up a pamphlet from the shelf. An expanse of pinkish leg and calf peeked through the split up the long black skirt she was wearing. I was looking at her when she glanced back over her shoulder at me.

The gentleman stood in the middle of the room. Mrs. Keating stood in front of him, adjusting his lapel. "Our Mr. Ferral, straight from Wall Street. How have you been," she asked.

"Not bad. Retired. Dull as hell."

"You're staying out of trouble, I hope."

"I am. About the only one."

"Oh," said Mrs. Keating, her chin back, studying his expression.

"They're all corrupt," he said, firmly without being loud. Mrs. Keating leaned back and looked at him. "All they want is money. They don't care." He nodded, looking at Mrs. Keating squarely.

"Yes, well, I hope not all of them," Mrs. Keating said, drawing a frown across her face, her brows raised, eyes open all the way.

"Money. That's all they care about now. Wasn't like that in my day. I couldn't stand it any longer, the way they act," the man said. The old man looked around the room.

I looked back at the Princess to see if she were listening. There was a rapidity now to the way she leafed through things, putting them back on the shelf. She looked over her shoulder at me again then turned abruptly back to the shelf, picking out one more folder.

"No morality at all. We'll see it all come out. Don't you worry."

Mrs. Keating had raised her eyebrows. "You don't say," she said, bemused. She glanced back over at me, almost with a wink. "Are you staying up for the weekend?"

"Yes, I think I will," the old man answered, nodding crisply.

"That's marvelous," said Mrs. Keating, beaming.

The old man nodded, checked for something in the breast pocket of his suit, and then wandered away, looking around curiously all the while. I was about to get up and go over to say hi to the Princess. I rose from my seat. A cold look came over her. I was standing now. I walked over to her. She tossed her head back and walked past Mrs. Keating's desk into the next room where the long tables were. I walked slowly over to the room. She had picked some literature off a shelf offering junior year abroad program information on the far side of the table in the middle of the room, and had turned to face me as I came in through the open doorframe.

"Going away next year?"

Silence. She turned the pages of one pamphlet with quick anger, flicking over a page in a way that reminded me of the tail of a cat about to fight. She stood still a moment. Then she put the pamphlet back on the shelf quickly, to hide it so I could not ask about it.

I turned toward a shelf, close to me, to my left. "France," I said with my old high school French accent, greeted by more silence.

Her head turned from side to side slightly, as if she was still looking at something before her. She would not look at me.

I bowed my head and walked back into the other room across the carpeted floor to the water fountain with the upside down three-gallon water bottle. I poured out two paper cone cups of cold water. I turned back to her but she had enlisted Mrs. Keating's attention and pretended not to notice me as I approached, standing there with two little paper cone cups of water. I sipped from one cup, holding the other in my hand.

She went with the woman back into the other room. I finished the second cup of water so that I wouldn't have to dump it into the trashcan. I put the crumpled cups into the small trashcan beside Mrs. Keating's desk. I sat back down in the chair and pulled one of the big black book of alumni listings back onto my lap. I looked down, listening to the pitch of the voices in their conversation.

Finally they came back into the room. Mrs. Keating was back at her desk, standing for a moment, then sitting down to write out a note about an item she would investigate for the Princess. "Yes, I remember now," Mrs. Keating said, checking something on a notepad through her half-glasses. In the middle of doing so, she turned to me. "Well," she said grandly, with an attentive smile that surprised me, "what did you think of our Mr. Ferral? Isn't he marvelous."

"Yes," I said. "He says they're all corrupt," I said, barely looking up.

The lady had turned to me, leaving the Princess standing on the other side of her desk. "Yes, he did say that, didn't he," she said, still ignoring the Princess. She smiled at me. I looked up at her, my chin down in the book still, offering a smile back to the woman, who continued to look at me.

"You know, I changed my mind," the Princess said in a high capricious tone, not willing to be ignored. "I'm not interested."

The woman turned in her chair back to the Princess. "But I thought you were," Mrs. Keating said.

The young woman turned quickly toward the door.

"Okay," Mrs. Keating shrugged, discarding the note she had begun to write on, turning to the far side of her desk.

The girl left the room. The older woman turned back around and looked at me again. I felt her smile gently at me. I sat with my arms closed in on the big book, as if to protect some silly dream, some dream I knew was a lie to have, that I wasn't going to bother with anyway. I was just reading about people and "what they do all day," as Richard Scarry put it. Mrs. Keating turned, adjusted her jacket about her comfortably, and touched her phone, as if expecting a call about the end of the day.

I stared silently into the page of listings before me, not finding anything. The woman rose with her half reading glasses in hand to check something in a different room around the corner. I quietly closed the thick book with a computer-paper thump, put it back on the shelf behind me and slipped away.

That night the television room up at the house was empty. I turned the television from the sports channel to PBS. There was a television show on PBS about the *Luftwaffe*. I sat back and watched the flickering TV screen.

There was a picture of the man reputed by his ranks to be the handsomest flier, a quiet man famously liked by all his fellows. The still black and white photo showed a man in his leather fleece-lined flying jacket, looking halfway to the side with a gentle smile, half beatific, a German Gary Cooper, like the picture of Lou Gehrig bowing at the microphone. You could tell he was a decent guy, a good sense of humor about him, that he wasn't a scheming s.o.b. like a lot of people turn out to be.

I looked at the television, sitting up from the sofa. Then they were talking about a new fighter plane, the first jet. In black and white footage, the little plane cooked down the runway and up into the air. They rushed testing to get it flying before the Third Reich was finished. There was a fire on the runway.

I watched now an interview with the test pilot, survivor of the fire. The show had a long interview with him, the man speaking out of his burned surgically rebuilt rubbery mouth. I could hear him speaking German on the audio, the translation over it. I looked at his face, a flat blank mask, no nose, no lips, hardly a brow. I made the connection.

I went to the bathroom after the program was over. I stood in front of the mirror looking at my face in the light.

I came out the side door of the Chapel. The snow was falling out in the quad and the air was clean, sharpening my nose. There was light way up above a moving gray band of cloud and silver space. I walked down, out to the middle of the quad.

We'd just brought to life with the old man a Keats poem, When I Have Fears. I'd finally got it, seen how every piece of it fit in. The flakes came down now, touching my nose, my face as I looked up, with tiny kisses of disappearing wetness. The ground was hard, the small ruts and tiny bumps firm against the foot, and I was satisfied by that too, as I was by the cold light coming golden through the clouds shining on the bark of the trees standing there and the expanse of the valley below receiving the coming snow.

Our parents carry poetry within them. They are too busy, too much a part of it to question the basic and natural assumptions that have shaped their lives. They work on quietly, keeping the poetry about themselves, as if by silent sounds of a sea they do not question.

In quietness and solitude we capture that poetry, as to show it to others by whatever means we may be given. And if they should not understand at first, what are we to do, but continue on our way, stronger.

And every boy, in his own mind, wants to be Shakespeare, that the prose of life and the mundane has its poetry, rightfully so.

CHAPTER TEN

Duchamp's class on Contemporary Cultural Criticism was up on the third floor of the old Converse Library. Today we were talking about the music of Bruce Springsteen. Duchamp thought we would have more to say if he left, and so he had picked up his folder-like briefcase, stood up and left, closing the door behind him.

No one said anything. A few looks around, a couple of silent giggles.

"I think these songs are saying, 'Yeah, I fucked up. We all make mistakes. I'm trying the best I can,'" I said. I had listened to the latest album on the truck radio that summer. Kenny had ended up with the blond from the cleaning crew one night in a car at the Vernon Fair at summer's end.

Tom Boone, seated next to me, nodded. A short kid slouched in his chair stared at his wire-bound notebook, a blue plastic pen lying on top of it.

After class I went up to the chapel to talk with Duchamp. He wanted us to clear the subject of our final papers with him.

"I was thinking of two things for my final project, either doing it on James Dean or Ernest Hemingway."

"Either would make a good study about cultural phenomena, about what society reveals of itself through its language, its attitudes, its treatment of an artistic persona."

Soft light came in through two windows through half open white curtains, one beyond his desk on the side of the building facing the dormitory South, and one behind, looking out on the portico. The room was perfectly quiet.

He looked over the materials on his desk, his chin down, a sweep of hair across his forehead, looking as if he was about to restrain a burp.

He nodded, and looked up at the wall behind me for a moment as he leaned back. "We live in a society that does not acknowledge selflessness."

He looked over at his piano, squinting at it as if he heard something.

I was looking down at his desk while he spoke. He took his glasses out of a sleeve. "I really wouldn't recommend trying to be a writer these days. The odds of making it are so long, and the reward, so little. The work entails a basic disagreement with the order of things. That's the only way you'd find time to do it, or be able to justify it to yourself. Otherwise you have to look out for yourself constantly." He shook his head. "It's just a painful set-up."

"I guess so."

He put his glasses on, opening a manila folder on the desk in front of him. He turned on the shaded lamp that sat on his desk. "Well," he said. His desk faced the opposite direction as Carlson's. It just felt different, and there was the light coming from the portico behind him. The room was cluttered, and you felt the piano behind you, an instrument to make sense of it all. And I was glad to be able to sit there for a moment, me and him, in silence, just the light.

"Nothing is, but thinking makes it so, our friend Hamlet says," he added, without looking up. "Maybe you'll find that some inspiration comes from being unselfish in a selfish dog-eat-dog world." He looked up at me, his eyes enlarged by the lenses of his glasses, with what for him was a wry kind of smile, just as his vocalizations could not fall into the conventional categories of ohs, ahs and ums.

"Thank you, sir," I said very quietly, and the man said nothing in response, pulling his chair forward slightly, peering down into the stack of papers before him, familiarizing himself with their content.

I stood, closing the door behind me carefully, glancing back at him sitting there absorbed. The desk was a good distance from the door.

The rain was falling across the windshield. "Easter is not about bunny rabbits and the coming of spring. It is the most meaningful of the Christian holidays, as important as Christmas. I wonder if these local hack ministers like Frank Schlitz really understand the significance of Easter, of Christ's rising. But then it's not given to everyone to want to understand the nature of reality."

The windshield wipers swung over the windshield steadily, the pellets and droplets of rain pushed away by the hands of a helpful wind. We drove along across the floor of the valley, the sky low and dark.

"Jesus Christ returns in the body of light, a manifestation of the higher reality, the true being of man's soul, which He represents in His acts while alive in the world," my father told me. "The Cross is symbolic of Christ the higher reality, the true soul, coming to the dimension of the world we see around us. The Cross is a cube opened up along its edges and laid flat, to reveal its nature, that of a three dimensional object, to the reality of two dimensions." My dad paused and we continued rolling along the same

slightly rising road to Utica we'd gone on a thousand times. "An object from a higher reality, manifested in a lower reality."

"Dad, does the Cross mean that we'll suffer?"

"Yes, Jamie, in every life there is suffering, just because we are alive in this corporeal world."

We drove by a roadside church, a low brick structure with a high steeply angled roof. "Now the popular image of Christ is one of meekness and love for all, a sentimental image that these local yokel ministers like, as it keeps everyone calm and no one has to think too much. But Christ's acts were informed by a particular sort of knowledge. His acts were not random acts of kindness and decency." My father, with his bald spot and occasional jerk of the neck to shake out the stress of being intelligent in this world, looked over and I nodded.

"Christ could be angry too, not just meek and defenseless as he is sometimes made out to be. He tips over the tables of the moneychangers in the Temple with His own hands. He casts them out of the Temple, and it is for this as much as anything else that brings the high priests against Him. The rules of society are offended when you reach beyond them, when you reveal the error of judgments.

"As Christ enters Jerusalem on Palm Sunday He is carried on a donkey, 'Brother Ass,' the donkey representing the earthly body that carries around the soul. Christ knew what was going to come to Him, as each event fit within the meaning of His existence in the world. Finally, in His resurrection, in coming back to His earthly companions, the Disciples, Christ establishes His relationship to everyday life as the higher true reality within

mankind. He returns in the body of light, to show dramatically what He represents."

"So, this body of light reveals our own real nature to us."

"Yes. And also the nature of reality around us." And looking forward watching the road before us, my father, wearing his Irish cap, nodded again and I felt very satisfied and glad that it was spring and Easter time.

"And in some way we too can see things happening, if they have something to do with our souls?"

"Yes. If we don't see that nature, that day-to-day reality has meaning and shape behind it, then we miss understanding what being in the world is all about.

"Not everyone can handle that, but yet someday we all come to that understanding," my father said, leaning over slightly. He looked up the road. There was the rain and moving forward and being alive. And I responded as I always have and always will respond to something that is good and true, which is to understand, agree to and take to heart.

I crossed Main Street, and walked across the grass up the long yard in front of the old Phi Gam house toward the hedgerow. I thought about Christ standing in the garden in the morning light, appearing to the woman, Mary Magdalene. She was probably an attractive woman. They loved each other, otherwise she wouldn't have been the first to come upon Him. She was faithful to come to His tomb in the early morning. Did they embrace? It makes no difference if they did, because he had come back, in the Body of

Light. But maybe because His body was now made of light it would be impossible to touch him. Then is our higher nature impossible to touch?

On Easter morning the two shone together, in humility, in adoration, and she had become like him, and their bodies of light met in ecstasy, sharing each other, discovering each other's similarities, and how they could shine together in a certain special way. Yes, they made love, in the morning, on Easter. For Christ had risen and Mary Magdalene had come to him, and she was good too. He was a man, shining, and she was a woman, enveloping him, shining too.

Peter's mom came out from Boston that night, Good Friday, to take us out for dinner to celebrate his birthday. We went to a Chinese restaurant in an alleyway off of the main strip. I sat and sipped a beer, listening, eating with chopsticks. The dining hall was closed by the time we walked back, all the chairs pushed in. Another chance, another miss I had to live with in this thing we call time.

I looked for the Princess at the dining hall Easter night. She was nowhere to be seen.

At ten I went to meet Hersh for a beer at Fayerweather. I ordered us a pitcher, and brought it back to a table in the middle of the room. I brought the chilled glass mug up for a sip.

Hersh looked around me without craning his neck, leaning slightly. He pointed silently with a nod of his chin. I turned to look down my arm at the ground. The Princess had walked in with her friend Daria. They slid into a wooden booth on the raised platform above the shiny hardwood floor.

The Princess swept quickly to the main room, returning with a grilled cheese sandwich on a white plate, the slice of tomato peeking out brightly beneath the browned top. She placed it down as she stood and sat back down in the booth, looking away. She raised one half of the sandwich and delicately bit into the corner, then raised her eyes back at the girl across from her. The little girl on the other side of the table began to speak. The Princess placed the half of her sandwich back on the white plate, and gave her reaction, skeptical about something, her tone high-pitched, excited for the time of day. I could not make out a word of what she was saying.

Hersh poured us two more. I sipped the foam off of the beer before it ran over. Something crossed Hersh's face as he monitored her lecture in the background. He leaned back and exhaled, looking back at me, rolling his eyes.

The opening piano phrase of *That's Just the Way It Is* came out from the jukebox. I looked down into the goldenness of my beer.

The Princess had finished her sandwich and kept on talking, the little girl listening, holding her ankle, one leg crossed over the other. I finished my beer.

I got up and used to the phone in the hall to check in on B-Dorm. She came quickly out of the broad opening to the back room of the snack bar, buttoning her jean jacket, her girlfriend walking by her side. She stepped down the wooden stairs, tossing her hair back, passing with quick steps to the back exit, pushing the bar of the door open with two hands before her, the shorter girl following. I went down the steps slowly and stood outside the door. I looked down the hill. They stopped before the light of the entryway to her dorm, turning to face each other, standing still.

The light behind her, I saw her in profile. She turned and looked back up the hill briefly, a half dozen juvenile trees of different heights on the slope between us. She turned to face her friend. I could not tell if they were speaking. They could have been whispering, or they could just have been standing there to see what I would do.

I stood for a good minute. No one moved. I whistled the call of the Mourning Dove, repeating it. She stood there, facing her friend in the darkness by the light above the door waiting.

I stood there next to the tree. Another long minute passed. Her friend turned, and I just barely heard "good night." Then the Princess turned slowly, her head bowed slightly. She stepped up onto the landing into the light, then in through the glass door. I turned and walked away.

The next weekend the New Dorm threw a keg party. I had a few beers in my room and walked down. The dance floor was crowded. I went and stood by the lone window along the side of the room. I glimpsed the Princess out on the dance floor, not looking one way or another, dancing in an aloof manner.

The DJ played a song everyone liked. "*Yesterday I felt so old,*" the crowd sang along with it. I went out onto the dance floor. I took a step toward her and the slight kid with dark hair she was vaguely dancing with.

She moved toward me instantly, raising both of her arms out, pushing me with her hands abruptly so that I took a step backward.

The slight kid became more animated in his dancing, defining his presence with her. I stood still for a moment, the thumping opening beat of *White Lines* throbbing out from the speakers at the back of the room. The kid backed into the space close by my left. I moved my elbow out to let him know. He bumped into me with his shoulder, amused. The kid turned away, keeping his eye on me. I looked at her for a brief second, at her ignoring my presence. I took another look at the kid again. I left, not talking with anyone, walking back up the hill.

Monday, I came down the hill from the library past a stand of dogwoods along the back of Converse. I saw the Princess coming up the walkway, wearing a look of distance, practicing her New Yorker walk.

I stepped in alongside of her. She concentrated her look forward now. A tightening of amusement rose up her body. She nodded her head up slightly, still not looking at me, smiling through her refusal to smile.

She looked forward without saying anything, trying to stifle the pleased vibration that passed through her. She walked briskly to the doors of the mailroom. I got there a step before her. I opened the closer of the two doors with arm out to let her pass inside. She passed in through without saying a word.

I waited outside. Five minutes passed, and then finally she came out. There was another way to get out, by going upstairs, but she came back and looked at me, trying to put on a "oh, you're still here" kind of a look that looked slightly but well rehearsed. She had regained control over her stern expression, her chin up slightly, assuming tunnel vision. She brushed quickly past me.

We went walked along the path to the front of the library, then set out across the lawn. She was heading to Diplomacy class in Morgan Hall across the road. I kept up alongside her.

"You're always following me," she said.

"I'm not always following you," I said. I was to her left. "Sometimes I'm on this side of you..." I moved ahead of her and looked back over my shoulder. "Sometimes I'm on this side of you..." I swung over to her right, singing as if in an opera, all the words in the same note. "And sometimes I'm on this side of you." I walked along, chin in the air, a lightly triumphant grin on my face.

"You're obsessed," she declared, keeping her pace even. She thought for another split moment, her long legs moving straight out before her. "You're obsessed with lots of people."

I leaned over slightly toward her. "Who else am I obsessed with?" I said quietly, looking around, confidentially, as if speaking to a shrink.

"Oh, I don't know," she said, her voice at a slightly higher tone. "But why do you... keep pursuing me?" she said. We were more than halfway across the yard, the old library behind us, the road coming closer. The lawn was green, slightly wet from the rain that had passed through in the morning. We stepped together a longer stride over the roots of the big old oak tree in the middle of the lawn.

"That's 'cause I love you," I said.

Her gate drew slightly slower. She pulled the leather shoulder strap of her woven straw bag back up to her shoulder, turning slightly away.

We came to the neatly kept wide road. She planted one foot and then another at the curb. I stopped to look both ways. She stepped forward into the road and across the other side, her head tilted slightly. I stood by the curb.

She walked up the granite slab steps. I watched her go in through the door. She was probably the last to get there.

I walked quickly to class, across the wooded quadrangle to the science center at the far opposite end. A light mist began to fall. I stopped for a moment to look at the Range through the opening in the trees.

Rain fell intermittently throughout the day. It was not warm out, and above all clouds sat upon our valley.

I got up the next morning and walked down. The sun was shining; there was not a cloud in the sky. The sky was blue.

I went to the library after lunch.

I got some work done on my final project and walked down toward B-Dorm to see what the boys were up to. The air was mild, a temperature you couldn't feel. Walking to the door, I saw her window. The window was open, the white vinyl window shade rolled all the way back up. Her window, I had never seen open, always closed. And now the light and the air, sweet and piney and like fresh water, came to the window and was let in. And I shone too. And I felt I was light again, coming to her.

That night the full moon came up orange over the town, sailing out above valley, turning golden, then silver as it pulled the earth with its wishes, commanding the sleeping to rise.

I went by her room about ten o'clock. I knocked on the door. No one came to the door and so I opened the door and crossed into the suite. I stepped down the stairs to her room. The roommate Laura was standing in the middle of the first of the two open rooms on my right. She pulled out a piece of paper from her denim jacket. She turned to me, standing motionless.

The Princess was sitting up in bed reading, propped up by a pillow, a bright light behind her, in a plain white tee shirt and boxer shorts. She was barefoot. She got up instantly from the bed, and came toward the open door.

The roommate came forward toward me. She came to the doorway, checking on the Princess. I reached out my hand and touched upon the sleeve of Laura's dungaree jacket by her wrist. I swung her arm just slightly back and forth once and then again.

"I knocked on the door a couple of times, but no one came, so I let myself in," I said, biting the corner of my lip.

I turned toward the Princess carefully, having waited a moment for permission, and something made me feel calm. "I just wanted to see if you wanted to go with me down to the Full Moon party down at the Zoo."

The Princess looked up at me carefully with a mixture of expectant curiosity and anxiety.

I swung my arm back and forth slightly, swinging Laura's arm a tiny amount again. A moment passed, no one saying anything.

"Leave her alone," Laura said firmly.

I looked at the Princess. "I just thought that maybe you needed a study break."

The roommate turned to me, her neck shortening slightly as her eyes widened, focusing on me, her chin shorter than the intensity of her Miss Manners etiquette. "Leave her alone," she said, louder, one half note higher. I let my hand drop from her sleeve.

I turned toward the Princess, who had raised her hand to the doorframe, leaning against it. She raised her head slightly, her eyes cast downward, listening to something far-off. She bit her lip slightly, her head turning slightly toward her roommate. Her roommate stared at me, having taken her arm back, standing up straighter. She swayed forward, turning her shoulders back.

"Well, okay. I guess you're busy," I said, looking back at the Princess. "I'm sorry I barged in on you."

I turned and went up the stairs, across the bare common room and out the door onto the landing. I closed the door carefully behind me, and down the stairs.

Then I was walking across the grass, wet and cool through my sneakers. I looked up at the moon. I walked across the silent playing fields, heading toward the moon, away from campus. I wanted her to see the stars, there Orion, with belt and sword. It seemed to say that we are all here for a reason, by design, by appropriateness, a gift of Heaven's love. Not that I'd ever have a job lined up, or anything like that. I just know the stars offer comfort and guidance, reminding you of a thought, that even if you forgot it for awhile, it would come back to you presently.

I saw her at lunch the next day. I was in the middle of eating a grilled ham and cheese sandwich when she appeared in the same room in the dining hall, the middle one of the three on the main floor. She came out with her tray and took a quick glance out into the room. She looked down at the salad bar before her. She took a seat by herself, facing away from me at a table by a window.

She slowly ate her salad, taking a pen out and writing something on a piece of paper she had by her side on the table.

I went up to her after I had finished my sandwich. "May I join you for a cup of tea," I said, the sun coming in.

"You say one more word to me and I'll go to the Dean and have you charged with sexual harassment," she said loud enough so that I heard it quite well.

I went over to where the coffeepots were and poured hot water into a cup, reaching for a tea bag. My hand shook slightly. I returned to the table where I was sitting with a junior guy who was a friend of mine, a football player from Milwaukee. I sat down, the blood running cold from my stomach up to my face. I looked at her, studying her back. She went to get up to get something, moving quickly, in the mode of making her point. She went back to her table, an alertness to her back.

"I'll see you guys around," I said, glancing down at my watch, a Hamilton military watch. She had made fun it once. When I stood I saw that she had gotten up. She bussed her tray and headed toward the foyer of the hall. I tendered my tray to the dishwasher behind the stainless steel window.

When I came up the hallway she bent down to pick up her woven straw carrying bag, which happened to be close to my own notebooks. Focused on lifting her bag up slowly to her shoulder--she was a picture of style and grace when carrying her bag—she looked down toward the floor. She paused, listening for something. Coming from behind her, I swept up my copy of *Islands in the Stream* and blue bound notebook.

"That's ridiculous," I said, quietly, my throat constrained into a tight space. She lifted her bag up on her shoulder, bowing her head as she turned without stepping away.

I walked away and out the door on the left, town-side of the hall.

The next weekend on Saturday night there was a party at Charles Drew. I saw her come in with a guy from her class who played on the basketball team. Handsome kid. Tall.

I pretended not to notice her. I went out onto the dance floor to be left alone in a corner.

There weren't many left now. The two of them came in and took up dancing in the far corner. The kid was either not enjoying himself, feeling used for something, or was simply had no rhythmic inspirations, for all his abilities dribbling and shooting out   and muscling his way around on the basketball court. Looking ahead at the room she came in and out of my sight. They came out of their corner. He did have a confident look, even if he was bored out of his mind or whatever it was, something fatherly, I guess, tolerant.

They edged across the room closer to me. They moved around together, her feet sweeping the floor, him trying to loosen something in his back. I saw a flash of joy, curiosity on her face. Then they were not far away from me. She had moved them that way. The room was nearly empty now. I'd look up and see her drifting closer.

I pretended not to see her. I stood dancing, not looking at her. Then I went outside for a little air, not really knowing what I was doing.

They left finally. I watched them through the panes of a glass door walking away along the dark street. The night was empty now.

I had been going to Prescott's class on 20th Century British Poetry all along, not missing a single class. I had stopped saying much in class. Two years before I would dutifully raise my hand and try to think aloud, though I was careful for trying to think first. Bringing in a family photo of our visit to Yeats's Tower when I was six was part of an old loyalty between us. The class was in the old geology building, in a lecture room with rows of folding wooden theater chairs. I found them hard seats to sit in. The first paper had been due a month ago. Prescott had just assigned us the second paper the previous class. There was a brief break while we flipped through our Thomas Hardy books to a poem involving crows.

The professor put his book down and took a quick step over toward my seat the second row over to the side. Prescott came up to the wooden chairs, putting his hand on the row below, holding several dialogues of critical thought in his mind. He leaned forward. "I never got your first paper," he said gently. (You could never qualify his hair, as it too was too clever and subtle. Like anything he said.) Perhaps some sort of mistake was to account for it. The second paper was due in a week.

"I haven't written it yet," I said.

"Oh."

"Maybe I can come by your office," I said. "Will you be there for office hours on Friday?"

"Yes."

"Okay." I sat back in the chair. They were hard chairs to sit in for longer than half an hour.

I swung the outer door open at the quadrangle entrance of the Chapel. Prescott's office was the first door on the right in the hallway. I passed through the entryway, two stone stairwells on either side. Prescott inhabited his office, his home away from home. The door was open a wide crack. I heard a few pecks at the typewriter from within, tap, tap, tap. I poked my head in.

The professor looked up from his chair and beckoned with his chin raised slightly. He kept the room dim, one lamp at the edge of his desk, no overhead light. The bookshelves along the wall were full.

I sat down in the chair that faced the desk, the manual typewriter.

"I gather you're having trouble getting your papers done," he said in a dry voice, as if to comment on a meteorological condition.

"Well, to begin with I'd like to write you three papers, I really would. The subjects are interesting, it's stuff I like talking about. But..." I shrugged. "I just can't write papers anymore. I've tried. I sit down. Nothing comes."

Prescott looked back at me without betraying anything.

"I just don't see it happening."

A moment passed.

"I've always treated second semester seniors differently," Prescott said, raising his voice calmly. "You'll have to hand me in something," he said slightly louder. "And you're not going to get a good grade, but hand me in something. So I can pass you."

I looked down at my sneakers.

"Anything pertaining to the class…"

"I can do that. It's not that I don't think about the poems. I love the Hardy ones, the one about the man who can't afford to keep his dog anymore. And everyone likes the Houseman. Good stuff."

"No, I can see that you do. I've never had problems with you before."

I rose from the chair. "Well, thanks for putting up with me. I'm sorry it's come to this. I'll get you something handed in."

"Okay." The professor turned to his desk, looking down at a piece of paper, lifting it, looking at what was underneath it there by the lamp.

I knew it from that first day in his class. Duchamp had passed around a mimeographed piece of paper, a single poem on it, Winter in the Fens, by John Clare. "So moping flat and low our valleys lie," the first line read. We sat there in the room, the tables placed around in a square, the sunlight crossing the room to the wall. He called on a funny-looking kid who blinked a lot sitting across from me to read it, and I followed along. It just reminded me of something, reminded me of everything. I knew then I was for poetry, more than anything else, for better or worse. Not knowing what that meant.

CHAPTER ELEVEN

The final class came on a warm Thursday in early May. Duchamp was taking us out to his house out in the hills. We met in the parking lot below the Chapel. I climbed in the front seat of Duchamp's yellow *Volare* station wagon, wood paneling along the sides, dried mud caked along the wheel wells. I put my feet down on the straw scattered about the floorboard.

"We can roll down the windows," Duchamp said, moving aside a pair of tan leather work-gloves from on top of the dashboard. The two girls in the back rolled down their windows halfway. The man looked back at them in the mirror, and they drew themselves up, noses toward each window, smiling back at him.

We descended the terraced hill leading out of town, sunlight dappled across the polarizing windshield. We crossed the open plain of Hadley, farther away from the high land of the Range. We passed stop lights, gas stations, green rows of corn plants just coming up from the brown earth, the shells of four old Triumphs waiting under tarps in an overgrown meadow next to a sagging farmhouse, its wood clapboards gray and bare, a cinderblock carwash closer to the road.

The pale brunette in the backseat asked him about his children. A daughter had graduated the year before.

"I went down to visit my son in New York in January. He's making films." The traffic slowed now, the bridge over the big river rising before us. "He had a pizza box taped over a broken window pane," he said with his dry drawl, shaking his head.

"I had a pizza box taped over my window this winter, too" I said. I broke into my room one night too drunk to find the keys in my pocket. "Same damn thing happened to me too," I said, turning around and nodding to the girls in the seat behind me. They didn't laugh. Then we crossed over the river, a railroad bridge upstream reaching an island with little cliffs. The river was brown, a ripple by the pilings. The bridge rose up and then dropped us down toward the overpass of 91.

We took Route 10 into the hills on the other side of Northampton. Then we were in the country, the road surrounded by woods, shadows flashing across us at even pace. The road climbed into a conifer forest, then dipped, then leveled and then it climbed again. Below the road water ran in a streambed. The trees were tall and straight up above the two-lane road. We passed old settled stonewalls of round rocks of the fields, some of them lining pastures, some of them along woods. We took a turn-off, passing a sign for a state park, a glimpse of a waterfall through the pines down below the road. You could not see how to get down to the stream. "This is when they usually come down here to go swimming," he said. "Pretty cold still."

We pulled up to the end of the road, an opening in a row of sugar maples, a small stable before us, an open dirt turn-around, to the right two bare wooden houses, attached by a series of decks, all grayed in the elements. We stood around as everyone gathered and then we all went into the smaller, more angular of the two houses, an A-frame, with clean tarpaper shingles. There was a clean cedar smell beyond the transom. The walls were lined wit bookshelves filled from top to bottom. There were stacks of papers here and there, wherever they would fit.

We all sat around in a circle in the spare room, a skylight high above us, the old man directly to my left, his legs out straight, arms across his chest in a Shaker wooden chair. He looked a size to big for the chair, with a certain typical elegance that comes of a self-confidence and light. A guy in my class talked about fishing magazines. And then the man nodded to me. I was feeling a little sick almost, but an inner voice told me, 'do not be afraid, you have it all right.'

"Last at bat, just like Ted Williams," I said. I handed out the copies I made of the chapter excerpt. I read the passage from the book *Islands in the Stream*.

"A man draws a picture of a cat to get at the universal characteristics, the catness, of all cats. Here is Hemingway's character making observations about his cats. One likes to climb an avocado tree. Through his observations, the writer reveals something about human nature: we study things. Writing about cats, the writer is praying." I took a glance around the room at blank faces, silence, pre-skeptical, withdrawn.

"*The Old Man and the Sea* is a story that anticipates the events of Hemingway's own life. Hemingway goes back to the place of his youth to write about bullfighters. He finds a duel going on between two legendary matadors. As he sits down to write it he finds himself losing the ability to write. The design of his story of an aging fisherman, a great fish, and the attempt to bring his catch back to land becomes reflected in the events his own life."

I cleared my throat, raising an eye to look around the room again at sullen student faces. "The artist uses his life, as Hemingway did, to give us a picture of ourselves. We pray, in hopes of understanding the world, of understanding ourselves and the place we have in the Universe."

I leaned back in my chair, folding my arms. The students sat silently around the table, not sure of what to make of it all, the drive out, liberation from the classroom, the gradual enveloping of a more natural world, and now finally listening to the presentations. I had contributed a final puzzling piece.

Duchamp, his legs straight out before him, one over the other, bowed his head down, leaning forward. He put his hands on the tops of his knees. I waited for him to speak. His hand went up the back of his neck. He leaned forward, a slight clinch of the lips at the edge of his mouth.

"Mr. Tarnowski understands that there is a certain sort of verbal behavior in the response that a culture makes to a phenomenon. While it would have been kind of him to present some of those responses and compare them for us, looking for their particular meaning, he has given us a perspective outside and beyond those that attempt to categorize Ernest Hemingway as, say, a product, a brand-name that speaks of manliness and outdoor activity and adventurous bravado." He nodded, and that was it.

We rose and walked through another doorway out into the piney air again. A series of decks, at levels descending, lay between the two houses, extending out above the tall grass that sloped away down to the edge of the woods, like a great tree house. We passed through the sliding glass door before us. The lady of the house, a short flush-cheeked woman who reminded me about of someone out of a fairy tale, greeted us, offering us tea and muffins, a set of plates laid out on a long dark wood table unlike any I'd seen before. I took my cup, and stood there for a moment with the small crowd, the light on the treetops of the hillside.

I stepped toward the darkening window. Long shadows had come to the land below the house, passing over the boulders in the yard, the sun setting over to the right.

"My parents built a house something like this," I said, taking an oatmeal cookie. "There was a stream in the woods in back we'd hear at night when we went to sleep."

"Oh, that's nice," she said. "There's been a black bear crossing the bottom of the yard just this week." She looked out the window with me for a moment, and then I felt her back away, turning to a group of four standing by the dining room table.

I didn't tell her it was gone now. They had their house. No impersonal administrative force had come to mess with it. Nothing had come out of the past to protest the closeness of the walls. The woods were silent, and calm.

When we left I looked back at the two little houses connected by the decks that stood above the rocky hill and the woods that went on and on. There was an agreement about the place, a rule of quiet understood, something like a monastery, a ritual calm of quiet study and books on shelves.

And then we drove back. I sat shotgun again and the man said next to nothing as he drove the car, looking out ahead at the road, the habit of the countryside entering him.

We came down through Northampton, over the bridge, past Stan the Vegetable Man, the wooden scarecrow cutout in front of the produce stand.

The old tobacco barns swung past, then the barren strangeness of the flats, an abandoned greenhouse complex to the left, an empty lumber yard on the right, across the road a stand of posts with vestiges of white paint off in the middle of a field, the drive-in movie theater where I had cried and slept through *Doctor Zhivago* when I was three. The Holyoke Range rose untouched beyond the vacant cinderblock malls.

He pulled the car up to the parking spot on the Chapel-side of the old yellow Octagon building. I watched him as he climbed the steps of the Chapel, opening, disappearing behind the door. And I walked down toward the town, past the statue of Henry Ward Beecher the preacher and the great larch tree that whispers with its limbs and softest needles, I felt clean and upright beneath my nervousness. The town lay before me.

And without really realizing it so much, and feeling a particular kind of lonely awkwardness of first steps, I had uttered my first real sermon, small, humble, largely unnoticed, speaking above the heads of the small bird-like gathering. It was a bit of a failure as far as answering a particular question, and yet it was an organic response, and it was no longer for me about a simple assignment anyway, but about a boy who loved an old fisherman and the things they shared together in life's classroom. The old man was not someone who found it easy to be touched, being rational and precise, critical and ever vigilant about the coached and hidden meaning of words. It was my parting word to him, a token of my deepest respect and gratitude for having made me who I was going to become.

No one came to pat you on the back, but nor did you want them to, for you were teaching them something valuable they would then go and think about. You felt a bit out of place, but it was good because you had started something and other things would lead from it.

No one, I suppose, wants to be a spiritual genius, for fear of the implications it might have to a life. But yet the insights build, and intelligence grows in a certain way, observing the great geometry of joy and sorrow, love and kindness, an even-sided triangle by which to make sense of human action.

You go with your strengths, whatever they may be. Maybe you want to apologize for dragging things onto a different plane entirely, one people don't often--almost never--touch upon in conversation. But it hurts more to not talk about the things than it does to bring them up, even if they look at you funny and think you are merely pursuing some strange tangent.

Even that sorrow that comes of being misunderstood is one of those quiet joys, a signpost along the road.

The ball comes toward you through the confusions of life and society, and you swing the best you can. Maybe you are a failure at it for a time, but you keep your eye open and try again, and then one day you hit the ball. You get behind it fully, make contact, and then you run with it. A terribly tender feeling comes to you, and you understand everything, how each note, each leaf fits in to the scheme as a whole. How to explain it in a way that people wouldn't distort? You do the best you can. You try to understand people, even if they don't understand you, for that is just a part of them.

No spiritual genius would take a path that has already been set, or be quick to fall into a camp. A genius would look at the problem, and do the math, and come up with a model he thought worked. And what had before been the place only for miracles and God, the Earth at the center of everything, became now part of science, personally understood, the heavens demystified, made sense of in their motions, as a poet is capable of as much as the scientist, the scientist in his models being something of a poet anyway.

Maybe they'll laugh at you, shun you, treat you as a deviant, but you know that's what your own sense of humor, your gentle understanding of people, is for. You can only do it all by being passive, and that isn't exactly a popular way to go about personal affairs. There is something, however, to be said for it.

It didn't hurt if you had a beautiful girl to think about, for inspiration. Maybe she told you in secret ways you did not consciously grasp that she listened to you, that you were indeed her gentle teacher she would be most proud to offer herself to quite happily, even if she was not allowed to say so. It was nice to have someone you would want to teach. It was like the simple solution, the easiest step one will ever take, of no longer trying to be happy, and just be, rather than wanting things that wouldn't be as expected.

The great beautiful surprise was how gentle you were, and the great force, stronger than anything that lay within that. If they thought your authority was that of a poseur, what can you do? They were bound to the notion, until you liberated them, setting them free to be good and unselfish and all they were afraid to be.

For you had not believed really, or expected as much, when you began either, and still the light had shone and you saw all that was distraction. Who knows what the reward is, you don't do it for anything, but because it is simple truth as far as how things operate.

The last day of classes I went into town and picked up the flowers I had ordered and took them the back way up to my room.

I left the house in the late afternoon passing under the hemlocks of the Dickinson houses, a soapy smell by the rhododendrons and the elms shading the street.

I crossed the road by the railroad bridge. I went in through the basement. I climbed the three flights to the top floor.

I knocked. The door opened. The Princess stood there. She glanced at me.

"Hello, Miss Dorfmann."

She did not say anything.

"Well, it's the last day of classes..." I said.

She moved her body to make a sigh.

"And I wanted to bring you..."

I moved forward into the room. I stood in the middle of the room, holding the flowers.

"I just wanted to bring you these," I said quietly.

She stopped and looked at me for a second, and then she turned.

"I don't want them!" she said, moving back toward the door.

I followed her toward the door and put the flowers down, leaning them up against the wall, the big picture window to my right. A demure plastic pink flamingo stood frozen on one leg just inside the window next to an elongated potted plant with a green frond at the end of it.

"Well, give them to your roommates then," I said.

I heard her take the bundle in her hands, the paper wrinkling as she grasped it.

I turned and watched her pick up the bundle, her legs straight, her back bent. Then with the bundle in her hands she turned toward the door, taking a light sideways step. She hesitated the tiniest of moments. She looked down at the package.

She held the bundle now, straightening herself after lifting it. Fusia peeked through out the sides where the paper was taped upon itself.

She reached out for the doorknob and began to pull on the heavy door, leaning backward quickly, her feet planted. The swinging weight pulled her forward a step.

I moved toward the point of her effort, reaching my arm around behind her to help her hold the door open. I found myself close to her. I sensed her breath, the infinitesimal wind about her, the light scent of her skin, the movement of her hair. I felt the easy immediacy our bodies had next to each other, my height measuring against her. Our shoulders almost touched. I felt the light and the energy of the world flowing through her. She was filled with it, enjoying it, and it was wonderful to see.

"You're Crazy!" she shouted, enunciating it carefully in a high tone. She leaned forward to set the flowers down outside the door on the landing.

As she did she looked down, to take in the object before her, as she had not looked at it and found a curiosity for it.

In that moment of leaning forward, I had a flashing impression of quietness come over her, an attentiveness in the cast of her eyes as she looked forward, a peaceful vulnerability to her cheek as I went past her like it was part of a dance.

"Crazy to bring flowers to a beautiful girl," I said quietly, the last word abbreviated.

She laid the package of fresh flowers down on the polished tile of the landing, bending at the waist. She stood back up as I held the door. She looked down, without saying anything, and I stepped forward. I moved past her, taking my arm from the door, letting it close.

I reached down to pick up the flowers. I heard the door swing shut, a faint groan as if to push something out a window. I held the bundle in my hands. I turned back toward the door. I heard the lock click. I bit my lip.

I looked down at the paper-wrapped bundle in my hands. I shrugged at the door. I blinked my eyes at the door, and there was silence from the other side of it, as well as silence around me. The door was polyurethaned wood. Everything else was something like tile or fiber, plastic or composite metal. The lighting above was fluorescent, set into fiber ceiling tile. A chemical smell of janitorial mop covered vague silt dust in corners. Everything seemed an odd surface, to have a strange kind of solidity. Had the floor tiles been made of tiny pebbles polished to shine?

The vibrations of the universe came shining at me, filling me with breath. My whole body shimmered with light.

I raised my hand to knock, and then I put my hand down. My mouth moved as if to make a sound, but nothing came out, and I pressed my lips back together. A vocabulary did not exist.

I turned and peered down the stairwell to see if anyone was coming up. I took the steps quietly and slowly, carrying the flowers in the crook of my arm down the steps. I turned at each landing, coming about, down the three flights of stairs to the basement door.

A dumpster sat outside the basement. I lifted the broad metal lid a crack and lay the bundle down on top of a pile of garbage bags next to an empty box of laundry detergent, the purpled pink folds of lilies visible where the paper had been folded and taped over. I let them go. I looked down at them. Then I let the lid back down gently. It creaked, metal rubbing against itself, closing with a metallic clank. The stale odor of plastic garbage bags and emptiness rose like an exhaled breath. The freshness of the flowers was gone now.

I walked away up the narrow road behind the dorms. The road was shaded, with pines on both sides. A robin watched me, flying up away into the branches of a tree not far above my head. I walked along like an idiot under the trees, stepping quickly, then slowing, then faster again. I felt the light was shining in me. The hair on my back stood, all goosebumps. I wanted to break into a run and a leap, but just walking along was a better way of hiding it.

I walked toward the playing fields, an opening of sunlight before me, a little hill of mowed grass. Some kids were tossing a Frisbee on the slope looking down on the fields. The girl, a blond with short hair—I had briefly dated her girlfriend, to my embarrassment—said hi and I said hi back.

I reached the field, the lacrosse scrimmage to my left. I went on further, along the outfield wall of the baseball field, the baseball players tossing the ball back and forth, someone batting, everyone doing separate exercises, with the same fluid movements as the robots of an assembly plant. I came up Memorial Hill, walking up the steepness of it bent forward slightly with long slow strides. I walked across the quadrangle, the freshness of air rippling through the new oak leaves. I decided to go to the dining hall early, right after it opened, so I wouldn't have to see her and she wouldn't have to see me. I wanted to be quiet, to hide all that was within me. Now I couldn't tell if it was some huge lasting sadness or what it was.

The dining hall opened at five fifteen, and I was with the first in line.

Tickets to the reggae band down at the old gym were on sale at a table in the entry. I was pulling a bill out of my wallet when I saw her coming in my direction. She slipped into the woman's room. I looked down into my wallet.

I left the dining hall and sat outside at one of the tables they had brought out for the nice weather underneath a tree a good way from the door. The late afternoon sun was casting golden beams upon the budding trees, and the trees seemed alive, as if they were about to stand up and walk somewhere. I sat silently, not sure how I felt or what I was feeling.

I saw her walk out a little while later. She looked over at me briefly, as if puzzled, questioning something in her mind, almost coldly, then turned back forward without expression. She walked away with her roommates down the hill toward her dorm, her chin raised forward, her eyes cast down.

I walked down Memorial Hill with a crowd of underclassmen to the concert in the old Cage.

The lacrosse team was selling beers from a keg. A friend of mine pulled out a bowl. I took a hit off it. I passed it back, holding the smoke in. I coughed, the bass thumping in my chest, the syncopated chord from the keyboard and guitars coming over it.

A very pretty sophomore stood before me, looking up at the stage.

"Hi, how are you tonight?" I half-shouted to her above the band.

She looked at me not quite blankly. "Do I know you?" she said, turning to the side and looking at me out of the corner of her eyes, puzzled.

"Yeah, you're friends with the guys up at Taylor. I see you at parties up there sometimes," I said slowly.

"Sorry, I don't recognize you," she said, turning her head to the side and then back, her brown eyes wide, her chin turned to one side.

"Oh, okay," I said. I turned away, rolling my eyes, stepping to the side and forward, past her.

"I'm sorry," I heard her say, lifting her voice slightly. I walked away into the crowd, not looking back.

Sunday I went down to watch the lacrosse match against Williams.

After it was over, I walked up to Pratt to use the pay phone out front to call my mother.

"Hi, Mom."

"Hi, Darling. Thanks for calling."

"Happy Mother's Day."

"Thank you. I wondered when someone was going to call me."

"I was just down at the lacrosse game."

"So I'm coming out, I've decided."

"Oh."

"I need a vacation. I talked to Joan and they're happy to have me."

"Okay."

I put the phone down. "Jesus Christ," I said. I went in and down the dark hall to tell Hersh how the game went. Hersh was sitting on his couch reading *The New York Times*.

"They pulled it out."

"I heard."

"My mother wants to come out next week." I looked over at the turntable sitting on a shelf. "As if I…" I let it hang there.

"That's when you should just be partying your ass off."

I took the Billy Bragg record from its cover, put it down on the turntable. There was a song I liked. The jangling guitar opening of run-on chords came on.

"Do you mind if I play it loud?"

"Go ahead," Hersh said.

"*Thinking back now*," Billy Bragg sang.

I was looking out through the screen of the open window when I saw her walk by, along the sidewalk, in the shade of the dogwoods, her skirt down to mid-calf. Her stride slowed as she came past, as if she were listening to the music to accompany the Sunday best she wore now, in perfect time for spring.

"*Thanks all the same,*" Billy Bragg was singing.

"What the hell is she doing out?" I said.

Hersh, sitting back in his comfortable chair, looked up at me, then out the window. He shook his head.

I stood there in the room. I didn't know what to think, nor what to do. If she could have done so, why not 'til now? It seemed like she only wanted to torture me a little more, and I couldn't take it, and so I just stood there. I should have just sat down on the floor. The sudden passive femininity seemed too incongruous, too much an act that would disappear by the time I got there anyway. That was how I felt. A pang of pessimism, a lack of faith, as usual, at the worst time. Or maybe just a reciprocating of how she was with me, in our foolish little battle that went on and on without going anywhere. A moment of despair. I was not, apparently, the teacher I wanted to be, even if I wanted to be so. Maybe it just wasn't yet my time. Maybe it was simply that this was something bigger than any one person.

There is special providence in the fall of a sparrow. If it be now, 'tis not to come; if it be not to come, it will be now; if it be not now, yet it will come. The readiness is all.

I took Hersh's guitar from its case and took it out on the patio. I strummed some chords. I could see both paths on either side of the dorm. She did not come by again. I took the guitar back to the room.

I walked into town. I did not see her. I walked back to the house to the small room in the back of it.

I thought I had suffered the worst when she had closed the door on me. I thought I could say to myself that it was all over then and leave it at that.

I wasn't going to go to the dining hall. I was going to skip dinner and just get drunk anyway I could. I was going to drink a whole bunch of beers. The only problem was it was Sunday, and all the stores were closed. I had a few *Ballantines* in the fridge.

So I sat back on my bed. I still didn't want to go the dining hall. The window was open and I smelled the mouth-watering tangy smoke of chicken being barbecued. I tried to ignore it, and then I told myself I'd simply walk over toward the house and see who was having the cookout. I didn't want to go to the dining hall that night. There was a small party lounging out on the grass around a hibachi and two coolers, the staff at the snack bar. The pretty girl, the one with the bike who hadn't recognized me, sat laid out comfortably on a blanket, propped up on her elbows. She had worked the line in the snack bar that spring.

"Hey, this guy's cool. You hungry, man?" the full-time guy with the beard called out from the grill as I passed slowly by.

I stopped and looked over. "Yeah, hum, a little bit."

"Come have a piece of chicken. We got plenty."

They gave me a plate and I sat down. "He didn't work with us. I thought this was only supposed to be for guys who worked at the snack bar," a tall precious kid said. I ignored him.

"Good chicken," I said to the bearded guy. I tipped the guy whenever he got a beer from me. "Thanks."

"Not a problem, my friend," the bearded guy said, standing over the grill, turning breasts of chicken amidst rising smoke with a nod to himself. "No problem at all." The corner of his mouth rose and he turned to his beer bottle, taking a quick swig off it.

I ate silently and slowly, trying to manage with the plastic utensils. The girl sat there in the sunshine on the blanket. I felt her looking at me, as if she read my mood and the cause of it. I could see her there ten feet away from me as she sat back in the sun, leaning on her arms, her long legs out straight, looking like Brigitte Bardot. I did not ask her about her bicycle. She looked away into the sun, her chin on her shoulder, her ear tuned to summer.

I ate my piece of chicken, wiping my mouth now and again, not wanting to have barbecue sauce on my face. When I'd finished it I got up, thanked the guy again. He was drinking another beer now. I walked away back across the parking lot, the light golden, bronzing the fallen pine needles.

I went back to my room. I lay down on my stomach, my arm folded under the pillow, and I felt sad as hell. In my head there was a lake, half-filling it, and things began to flicker across the surface of it, things eternal, puzzling, that only I could understand, and I went toward where there was peace. If that's where your art takes you, that's where you go, something seemed to say, and I could not judge.

Then it was dark out and my mouth felt wet at the corner just above the pillow. I was looking upward from the bed. Then I heard a young woman's voice by the phone on the wall outside my door. She began to laugh. She laughed out loud. "Well," she said, laughing again, "it's like this schedule on someone's door. It's like… it's got all these things on it. 'Fuck you, you assholes,' it says across the blank where you write your name in at the top. Then it is has what this guy's doing from ten to eleven on Monday. 'Jerking off,'" she said, with a whispered giggle. "'Rolling in vomit and broken glass.'"

Her voice had a sweet feminine register to it. I could tell she was attractive, the way she could control her voice so well, and you could hear her smile.

I lay there in silence, not moving, not quite making out what she was talking about. I thought it would be funny to go crack the door open and stick my head out and she could see for herself who it was. But then she hung up the phone and was gone.

On Monday exam week began. I walked over to the Science Center, the big pink brick box. I had a suspicion. I needed to go see the professor from Twentieth Century Physics. I stood before the directory looking up the office number. I made my way downstairs and walked the long hallway till he came upon the office. I knocked on the door.

"Come in, please," the voice within called.

"Hi, Professor Sampanatha. I came down just to make sure you got my paper. I slipped it in under the door but was afraid it might have gotten lost under a desk."

The professor looked at me, not getting up from his desk. He brought up an open hand and motioned me with his palm to sit down in the chair opposite his desk. I sat down. He swiveled in his chair slightly and looked out the window, a tight frown across his lip.

"I have been trying to call you," the professor said evenly, as if simultaneously trying to restrain something that was eating at him.

"Oh, yeah, that number was never hooked up. I just use the Plimpton House phone."

"Well," he said a little bit louder, clearing his throat, "I would like to ask you a few questions, to see if you understand what we've been talking about in class."

He looked steadily at me now, with big eyes bright against the darkness of his thick beard, perfectly still.

"Sure."

"You did not turn in a single worksheet and therefore I do not know if you were listening or if you learned a single thing," the man said with a slight lisp, his thick lips unable to evenly meet his teeth.

"Well, I did go to every class, and I did take notes."

The professor sighed, and looked around at his desk. He was fond of calculating things, and indeed enjoyed saying the very word, calculate, taking his mouth the shape of an entire story complete with beginning, nuance and ending, a living thing. The situation now was something he, the professor from India, had no measure by which to calculate.

"There are certain requirements to any class, and simply attending is but one."

He asked him a series of questions concerning the Theory of Relativity, about a beam of iron traveling on a train and under what circumstances would it be longer or shorter, which I managed to fumble my way through, the man leading me once when I stumbled for a moment. A forlorn expression came over the man.

"You deserve to be flunked. And under any other circumstances I would flunk you."

I studied him carefully, looking for a moment at the man's large baleful eyes.

"It makes no difference to me that you are a senior, none at all." There was a Venetian blind behind the professor's shoulder to keep out the afternoon sun. "Only because it is partly my fault am I not going to flunk you."

I nodded, my eyes open.

"And never will I let such a thing happen again," Professor Sampanatha added in a slightly louder tone.

"Well, I'm sorry. And thank you for being understanding," I said. It was too late to do anything about it now. "Just be grateful and get out while you can," I thought.

I left the Science Center with a hollow feeling in my stomach. It was sunny out still and I went to the steps of the library and leaned back with my shirt off. There was a light breeze, but in the sun it was warm. I felt tired and stretched out flat, finding m body oddly supported by the edge of each step. It surprised him that I felt so comfortable, that the edges were neither sharp nor pressing unevenly against my back. It felt as if fingers were holding me up, as if they were about to effortlessly lift him, like I was floating.

I lay there, only the sky above me, eternal, blue, far away, my body soaking in the energy of the light. I closed my eyes, hearing the students coming and going, foot steps up and down the steps. The library, my old haunt, had become a popular place. I listened to the distant voices, young people speaking of epic final assaults, outwitting the mounds of work and tests before them. The boughs of the pines along the front of the library swayed with airy whooshing noises. The stone steps of the library, warmed by the sun, held me up as if they had been designed to carry my bones.

I began to drift as if I was on a boat. I breathed in the pine. Then I was at the college cemetery back home now at Christmas time with my father to get the evergreen clippings. My brother and I crawled under the yew bushes where the snow hadn't fallen. Then I turned to look back at my father, moving about beyond the white-capped stained headstones. My brother and I were helping carry them back, laying them on the newspaper spread in the back of the old blue Volvo, then getting warm again in the car as the blue of dusk fell, the grains of snow blowing over the top of the footprints we had made. My father shifted the stick into reverse and began to back out, looking behind him. We drove down College Hill, warm in the car, then along the road back up to the house, taking the greens to the basement and putting them in buckets of water.

And it came to pass, that after three days they found him in the temple, sitting in the midst of the doctors, both hearing them, and asking them questions. And all that heard him were astonished at his understanding and answers. And when they saw him, they were amazed: and his mother said unto him, Son, why hast though thus dealt with us? Behold, they father and I have sought thee sorrowing. And he said unto them, How is it that ye sought me? Wist ye not that I must be about my Father's business? And they understood not the saying which he spake unto them. And he went down with them, and came to Nazareth, and was subject unto them: but his mother kept all these sayings in her heart. And Jesus increased in wisdom and stature, and in favor with God and man.

"Aren't your nipples going to get sunburned?" a feminine voice above me said, waking me abruptly.

I craned my head up, my neck stiff, my eyes blurry. A figure was standing over me. The sun had moved to the right, lower in the sky. The young woman was looking down on me. "Well, I guess that's just the chance I have to take."

The Princess's roommate Lisa came just then to the left side of the long granite steps. She came lightly up the steps closer than she needed to, looking down demurely. Trying to hide her own expression, she came up the steps and went past.

"I'm going to be doing an internship at a bank in Boston," the girl said. "And what are you doing?"

"I don't know what I'm doing. I'm just going to go home first," I said, squinting up at her face, the sun above. "Leave here with my chin up." I wiped the side of my mouth with the back of my wrist.

I went to dining hall just as it opened on Wednesday again so she would not have to see me. I sat at a table next to an open window. I ate slowly, looking out at the sun as it sunk toward the horizon. Three black girls sat down to join me.

"Hi," each of them said politely, nodding in turn, looking at me with their deep brown eyes. I had never spoken with any of them before.

They ate quickly. They were working on a project together. I looked up at them when they got up.

I sat there at the table, the sunlight coming across the trees in the evening sky far away over my shoulder. I stared out the window a long time. Far away, a bird called, high up in a tree.

I slid the tray over to the aisle side of the table. I stood up, rising up with my tray in my hands, balancing it. Daria, the Princess's friend passed slowly before me, eyes forward, followed by the guard dog. The Princess passed in front of me, her head bowed. I pressed my lip in my teeth.

I waited for them to pass, and then I stepped out into the aisle. I turned and walked my tray away from the windows back toward the dish window. I went in to the serving line room, took an apple from a big basket and walked out past the coffee station and the milk dispenser into the hallway without looking back. No one said anything.

The next day was rainy, warm in a humid way. I wore a white cotton button-up shirt, the gray blue pants from the old suit of my father's. I walked toward town to get a haircut. I crossed the street downhill from the old library at the corner with the stop sign I had hid behind once, waiting for her. An odd sensation came over me, as if I were being noticed, as if I were crossing finally into a state of being I had no control over. I walked on, turning before the town hall, looking once at the clock face of its tower.

I found the shop. Bob, the King of Leisure, had recommended it. The barber nodded tersely, motioning toward a seat in which to wait. I sat, pretending to read *Sports Illustrated*, waiting my turn in the chair. The barber, a jovial red-faced man, warmly received his regular customers, laughing at their small jokes.

"What can we do for you?" the man asked me as he put the apron over my shoulders, tying it behind the back of my neck.

"If you could leave it sort of long in front..." I said. The man said nothing. The man brought out a fresh pair of scissors from the blue jar of Barbasol, and in five minutes he had finished. I looked in the mirror. It was all hopeless.

I paid the man and left. I returned to my room and lay down on the bed, feeling horrible. I felt it in my bones, that she was gone.

Before dinner I walked past her dorm. I stopped and looked up at her window from a distance, the shade pulled halfway up, without any light on inside. She was gone. She was gone.

I went through the line and took my tray out and sat by myself at a table under a tree. Three of her roommates walked by as I ate. One looked over at me, saw me looking back, and turned away. They walked up the ramp into the dining hall. They did not come to sit and eat outside.

"What's up, Wildman?" Hogan called walking past me.

I smiled back at him instinctively at first, then groaned to myself, "Oh, don't call me that."

On the Common a fair was setting up. Workers were setting up the amusement rides, unfolding them from their transport wagons on the green grass. The fair came when I was a little boy. I remembered looking up at everyone, a candied apple and life was beautiful and lights spun and my brother was there. I sat down on the grass. A couple passed before my eyes, hippie outdoor types, speaking Spanish quietly to each other, gazing into each other's eyes.

I looked back at the glow of the house from the field above our property.

Up close the house was like a ship. I had hoped everything would get better so that we could keep the house. I thought that would be good for all of us.

But now there was just a big hole and no one ever living together again. Now you just fleshed out whatever else was part of that situation. Whatever else there was just was a part of that, not having a home anymore.

Maybe it was like being a captain, too, in that you just had to go down with the ship, as a matter of honor. And in some ways, that was the beauty of life, discovering your genius as the ship sunk, taking you down, and there from the bottom of the waves you would do some kind of work you always knew about but no one else did.

I looked down at the glow of the house cradled in the dark sleeping woods that had closed in upon the land, as if something of Beethoven was playing, and I saw how perfectly beatific it all was. Maybe no one else, driving by the house, could see, would know that it was. It was no particularly terrible situation in comparison to the suffering that people go through in the world, not at all, but it was a kind of gift by which I would understand, in a broader way, certain things about reality, and sad as they were, they were a kind of comfort to me, a gentle lesson, providing a recognition that I was learning something, and that I was independent in my gaining of my own wisdom, for which I was proud, and no one could touch, but learn, one day, from, through, me and my example and my teachings. It was, as one might have expected, all about the light.

My mother arrived late in the afternoon the next day, coming by bus. I walked down and picked her up where the Peter Pan bus stopped along the Common, not far away from Hastings Newspaper Store. We walked up the hill to the house.

"It's so nice to be back here," she said. "It's so beautiful this time of year."

"Jamie, are you all right?" my mother asked.

"Yeah, I'm fine."

"You look like Job."

"Oh."

"Are you sad that I'm here?"

"No, I'm happy that you're here."

"Then is there anything that's a problem?"

"No, nothing's a problem."

"Then try to act a little happier or I'm going to think I make you sad."

"Okay."

"Good, because this is vacation for me."

"It's just that if you let yourself be sad, then you don't have to worry about the burden of trying to be happy, and I guess that makes it easier."

The next day we met on the steps of the old library. We walked up to the geology museum. We looked at the large flat rocks in the basement with small dinosaur prints running across them. Back upstairs on the main floor I found myself before the saber-toothed tiger, spine and ribs, skull. A mammoth skeleton stood in the middle of the room behind a rope, towering over the skeleton of an Irish Elk, tall, with a great rack of antlers on it. I looked at it the elk for a while. There were no more Irish Elks anywhere.

"Let me take your picture," my mother said, returning from a corner of the room.

I groaned quietly, turned around and she took a picture of me standing in front of the dark skeleton, the flash going off. Then we walked back across the quad. We sat down on a bench, to the side of the steps of the library. We looked out over the lawn, at the opening in the pines, the Holyoke Range in the sunny distance.

"If you didn't want me coming out you should have said something," my mother said.

"It's not that." I looked forward out across the grass. Some underclass kids were throwing a Frisbee out in the middle. "I just wanted this week to absorb it all."

"Okay."

"I feel like I've been pushed around, like... like I'm not the dominant elephant and I've been pushed around by all the others."

I would never have thought at the beginning it would end with me sitting there with my chin in my palm, sort of like *The Thinker* statue.

My mom looked out across the quadrangle, the black oaks casting their long shadows on the grass. "No one wants you to do anything you don't want to do. We just want you to find what you'd like to do."

"But how can you go through life, always apologizing for yourself? I didn't used to feel that way."

I looked over to my left, as the glass door of the library swung open. Professor Duchamp came out of the dark leafy reflection of the things of the quadrangle, crossing the steps above us, coming down the first series of wide granite. He saw me stand, raising his brow in recognition, tilting his shoulders forward just slightly as he came toward us.

"I'd like you to meet my mom," I said.

"You've made a big impression on him," my mom said, looking up at him as she shook his hand.

"It's been a pleasure having him," he said quietly. He stood tall again and prepared to turn to go on his way. "I've let him down," he said, and then he stepped forward.

"No, you haven't, sir," I said.

He turned and stepped away, down from the curb. From his backside I saw him nod, turning his head slightly to the right to acknowledge something as he walked forward, head down again in thought, crossing the little roadway, then up the sidewalk that rose to the Chapel, drifting away.

That evening, the night before graduation it was raining steadily. The house behind ours threw the last party. Carmine passed me a bottle of champagne and I took a gug. My brother and I stood, the rain falling, coming down like a fine spray filtered through the pines towering above us.

In the night, with my brother breathing heavily, asleep on the floor, the rain pattered on the roof outside the window. I lay on my side awake in the darkness.

The light outside above the trees was turning blue and my mother was at the door. She came in with Egg McMuffins and orange juice. I took my shower, shaved and came back to my room to dress. The house was silent. Not even the sound of a distant shower running. My brother was still out cold. I put a white shirt on, and then the black suit I'd found at the Salvation Army. *Sangers Northweave*, it said on a patch on the inside breast pocket with a golden needle going through, then *Gary's* below that. I pulled on white socks, thinking of spats, and my loafers. I tied my tie, an old one of my father's, with stripes, and then I slipped my gown on over my head.

The rain had passed. I walked through the quiet town. On the lawn by the church the robins strutted, dashing forward on tiny nimble legs, then stopping to look around again, their beaks raised, breasts stretched forward.

I crossed the main road and walked up toward the library and the damp murmuring shrouded crowd gathered beneath the trees. I walked along the edge of the rows of chairs they had set out. I passed one of the Princess's girlfriends. I went to find my place toward the end of the line.

I stood there. The line didn't move. A girl near me had brought her German Shepard with her. She pulled his leash and he stood, his tongue balanced just so. The trees stood there, still, no sound in their branches. Then the faculty came through, walking two by two, a collection of different caps and finer gowns.

The line began to move, heading toward the War Memorial then around and back toward the rows of plastic seats in front of the seated families.

The President spoke, relaxed in his Englishman way. Then a classmate, a young woman got up and made her speech.

"A diploma is an eviction notice in Latin," she said, standing at the podium on a phone book, and everyone chuckled.

The honorary degrees were handed out and then it was time for the class to begin filing right out of their seats to the end of the row, left past the faculty, then up the steps to the podium to shake the President's hand and receive the diploma.

My own row began to move and I followed the guy in front of me.
The line stopped in front of the faculty as each name was called, and then I
stood before them. They sat firmly, removed, shrouded by their caps.
Duchamp sat impassively, without expression in the front row. I kept my
eyes forward.

The guy in front of me was next to go up the three steps. His name
was called.

"David Michael Stockton."

I went up the steps carefully. The President stood before me.

"Jamie Matthew Tarnowski," the Dean read out.

The President smiled, holding out the rolled diploma tied by a purple
ribbon. I reached for it, and took the light tube out of his hand, my hand
wrapping around it. A burst of applause rose from the audience.

The President stood beaming, shaking my hand.

"You're a good man," the President said, in his particular happy
purring Englishman's voice, smiling like the Cheshire Cat. "Good luck to
you."

"Way to go," a tall young black woman said as I came down the steps.
I tried to smile at her. "Thanks," I said.

"The sweetest guy here," I heard her say behind me.

I went back to my seat.

And then we filed out and into the throng of people in the quadrangle.
There was shade under the trees. My mom was waiting for me, and I
embraced her short light body, her arms around me.

Professor Demetrious came up and shook my hand, grinning broadly, lighting up a cigarette. I looked around and everyone was gone, the crowd drained out of the quad and down to the buffet under a tent, with hardly a celebration, as if nothing had happened, as if four years of learning had not happened at all. I stood there with my brother under the trees.

"Guess I got to turn my gown in," I said.

We walked down to the serving line. The girl I'd seen at the reggae show was giving out the tickets.

She looked up at me and smiled, looking at my brother and then back at me. "I've seen you everywhere over the last two weeks," she said, her bright eyes nodding at me.

"Yeah, it's been a fun two weeks," I said. I didn't know what else to say.

We went back to my room. I hadn't done much to pack. My mom found a letter I'd tried to write to her in the drawer of my desk. "What's this," she said. "Oh, nothing, Mom." My brother looked around, shaking his head.

Finally we had the little car packed. We drove out away down the hill and through the town, and carefully through the four corners and past the college and then past the meadows, over the stream by the mill and then the left off at an angle of Shay Street. We pulled in the little sloping driveway.

My mom and got out and went to the door to the addition of the little bungalow. She looked in through the screen. "Well, maybe they'll come back soon."

I went and lay out in the hammock, looking up through the new leaves of the old apple tree, the sky blue and far away above.

I closed my eyes and opened them, and my head felt heavy, as if the world were about to spin.

"Just be yourself," I told her once.

"Why don't you be nice to me," I'd said another time, passing her. She turned away and a smile came out of her, a hint of a blush on her cheeks, unexpectedly, as she looked off to the side.

You would simply hope, that people would understand you, all the things evident in your face and the furl of your brow.

Mom called and I rose to my legs and walked toward the car.

I opened the door on the driver side and got in and closed the door behind me. I looked over at my mom. The sweetness of the world around us, the sadness ever a gentle part of it, I smiled briefly back at her thoughtful smile. I looked down at the dashboard and started the car, and we drove away, leaving the town.

Made in the USA
Middletown, DE
06 March 2015